AKIN TO ANNE

"I went to Witch Penny to see if she could find me a mother and she told me to come here."

L. M. MONTGOMERY

Akin to Anne
Tales of Other Orphans

edited by Rea Wilmshurst

An M&S Paperback from
McClelland and Stewart
The Canadian Publishers

An M&S Paperback from McClelland and Stewart

First printing March 1989
Cloth edition printed 1988

Canadian Cataloguing in Publication Data

Montgomery, L. M. (Lucy Maud), 1874–1942
Akin to Anne

(M&S paperbacks)
ISBN 0-7710-6157-9

I. Title.

PS8526.055A82 1989   C813'.52   C88-094739-X
PR9199.2.M6A82 1989

Cover design by Gordon Pronk
Cover illustration by Greg Ruhl

The interior illustrations have been reproduced from
the original publications.

Printed and bound in Canada by Webcom Limited

McClelland and Stewart
The Canadian Publishers
481 University Avenue
Toronto M5G 2E9

Contents

Introduction

THESE TALES were written from the heart. When Lucy Maud Montgomery was thirteen months old her mother died, and her father sent her to live with his wife's parents, the elderly and strict MacNeills. Shortly thereafter he went to seek his fortune on the distant Canadian prairies, and the young girl was left behind to be brought up by relatives who had no notion that a child needed anything but the basic necessities of life. Montgomery's early journals give a vivid picture of a suppressed and stultifying existence, physically adequate but emotionally deprived. At fifteen, she tried living with her father and his new wife in Prince Albert, Saskatchewan, but things were no better there. The second Mrs. Montgomery expected her stepdaughter to stay home from school to do housework and take care of the baby. In spite of her love for her father, after a year Maud returned to the devil she knew best, life in Cavendish with her grandparents.

It is not surprising that Montgomery sympathized with orphans and children brought up by uncaring relatives and made them characters in many of her stories and novels; the best known, of course, is Anne, the winsome, scrawny child with the big eyes who taught Marilla Cuthbert how to love her. Anne lost both her parents shortly after her birth and, until she came to

Green Gables at the age of eleven, lived in a succession of foster homes and finally in an orphan asylum. Green Gables was a dream come true for her, although at first she received understanding and sympathy only from Matthew Cuthbert, Marilla's care being limited to Anne's moral welfare.

Most of the stories in this collection pre-date *Anne of Green Gables*. Indeed, we can look on *Anne* as the culmination of Montgomery's impulse to write about orphans and give their stories happy endings. Her longing for understanding of her own desires and ambitions led Montgomery to find sympathetic homes and families for her orphan characters.

The use of the word "orphan" here includes more than children. Of the nineteen stories in this collection, only seven are about the very young. There are school girls and boys alone in the world, lonely young working men and women, middle-aged people wanting someone to care for, and older men and women whose lives are empty of love and family. How has all this loneliness come to be? In Montgomery's day families were broken up not by divorce but by death. Death in childbirth, as Montgomery knew from her own experience, was common at the turn of the century. When a young mother died, the father could very seldom cope on his own. He had the choice of remarrying or sending his child or children to other relatives. If those other relatives could not afford to take more than one child, siblings were sent to different families, perhaps in different locations, often losing touch after a few years. A widow had similar choices. If both parents died (as did Anne's), neighbours or relatives, close and not so close, had to be relied on for help. If a child was lucky, the new home, even if not well-to-do, could be warm and loving. At the worst, the outsider was made a drudge, given only minimal clothing,

care, and schooling, and treated harshly. What Montgomery's orphans long for is love, not rich benefactors.

Today we are familiar with the expansion of families
that occurs from remarriage after divorce. Similar expan-
sions took place in Montgomery's time when surviving
parents remarried and had new families. There are many
step- and half-siblings in these tales. Some may be un-
sympathetic guardians with no love for their charges, but
others are lonely and long for the companionship of any
relative, no matter how distant. In just a few of the stories
we see these relations, for example: a teenage girl finds
an uncle, her mother's half-brother; a young boy runs
away from a severe guardian, his father's older stepsister,
and finds a home with the aunt of his cousin; two working girls are discovered and claimed by their deceased
grandmother's half-sister; a woman takes in her stepbrother's son; a poor and lonely school teacher turns out
to be the half-sister of a well-to-do young man's law
partner; a college girl finds out that she is the daughter of
a childless man's stepsister. These discoveries and re-
unions reveal a wide sense of kinship and the passionate
longing Montgomery's characters have for homes and
family love.

Their longing for love leads some of them into paths
that few today, perhaps, would choose to follow. On the
verge of her departure for New York to cultivate her talent
for drawing, Jane Lavinia gives up her dream in order to
stay at home and "cultivate Aunt Rebecca" ("Jane Lavinia"). Of course, Montgomery's talented characters do
not always sacrifice their artistic abilities for love. In "The
Little Black Doll," when Little Joyce's undemonstrative
grandmother is told the child has a great singing talent,
she suddenly looks at the child with new eyes. Little
Joyce "realized that this strange, stately old lady, who
never liked little girls unless they were pretty or graceful

or clever, was beginning to love her at last." This realization means more to the child than the discovery of her talent. Another talented child is Ted Melvin, an untrained violinist. During "Ted's Afternoon Off," he is discovered by a professional musician and adopted by him. Ted will have a career, but to him the future is bright not "so much because of the music – it's because I love you, Mr. Milford, and I'm so glad I'm to be always with you."

Careers seem to be in the offing for two of these talented youngsters, and we can hope that Jane Lavinia continued to pursue her artistic interests from her rural home. Careers differ from plain jobs, however, and it is easier to have more sympathy with Montgomery's "typewriters" (as typists were called then), shop girls, and struggling teachers when they seem willing to give up their jobs for love. Constance Foster, an embittered primary school teacher in the town of Taunton, finds her only living relatives during her summer holidays in the country. Love enters her life for the first time, love for a home and the people who live there. She writes to a friend: "I am going to stay home with Aunty and Uncle. It is so sweet to say *home* and know what it means" ("Her Own People"). A pair of sisters, Penelope and Doris, the former studying to be a teacher and the latter a "typewriter" in town, consider themselves misfits. Doris thinks of "Penelope's uncultivated talent for music and her own housewifely gifts, which had small chance of flowering out in her business life." Even a reader who is quite happy not to have flowering housewifely gifts can understand why these girls are delighted when adoption by the lonely half-sister of their grandmother changes their lives completely ("Penelope's Party Waist"). There is even more to sympathize with in Marcella Langley's plight. Marcella, with an ill younger sister at home who should be sent to the country if she is to have any hope of recovering, is working as an under-paid shop girl. Though abused and insulted by one nouveau-riche ex-shop girl for over an hour, Marcella manages to keep her temper, and consequently finds a protector ("Marcella's Reward"). This is not the only one of these tales in which Montgomery snipes at nouveau-riche snobbishness nor the only one in which she compares the city unfavourably to the country.

Only a few of Montgomery's stories are set in the noisy, anonymous city, where society matters only to the idle rich. Those of her characters who live in cities long for the country, or should go there for reasons of health, like Marcella and her sister. Most of these tales end in rural surroundings, even if they do not begin there. When Chester Stephens is looking for work, he walks from the town into the country, and is aware of how good it is "to breathe clear air again and feel the soft, springy soil of the ferny roadside under his tired little feet" ("The Running Away of Chester"). Chester is lucky enough to find a home in the country. So does Grace, a student at a high-school academy in town. In "The Story of an Invitation," her friend Bertha notices that Grace, who had planned to work in a store all summer, was "much paler and thinner than when she had come to the Academy," and thinks she "could not stand two months at Clarkman's." Bertha has her aunt invite Grace, rather than herself, for a summer holiday in the country so Grace can regain her health. The aunt decides to adopt Grace. The heroine of "Charlotte's Ladies" is surrounded by the country, but cannot get into it. She looks through two gaps in the fence surrounding her orphanage and sees views that call to her. From the first "she could look out on a bit of woodsy road with a little footpath winding along by the fence under the widespreading boughs of the asylum trees." From the second she "found herself peering into the most beautiful garden you could imagine, a garden where daffodils and tulips grew in great ribbon-like beds, and there were hedges of white and purple lilacs, and winding paths under blossoming trees."

Montgomery pictures homes in the country, homes loved and homes longed for. She shows us the farm where Chester hopes to find work: "He liked the look of the place, with its great, comfortable barns and quaint, roomy old farmhouse, all set down in a trim quadrangle of beeches and orchards." The lonely Constance Foster was attracted to the house where her relatives lived before she knew it was the home of her mother: "Such a picturesque, low-eaved little house, all covered over with honeysuckle. It was set between a big orchard and an old-fashioned flower garden with great pines at the back.... She found herself learning to love it, and so unused was this unfortunate girl to loving anything that she laughed at herself for her foolishness." For Constance, love of place precedes love of people, but both loves culminate here. When the other Charlotte in this collection goes on her quest for a mother, the Witch Penny sends her down to the harbour ("Charlotte's Quest"). "Halfway along the hill she came to the house, the grey stone house with the door like a cat's tongue, a house so grey and old that it seemed a part of the hill. It had a dignified, reposeful look as if it feared not what wind or rain could do to it." Behind that red door Charlotte finds the kind of life and love she craves.

Montgomery obviously prefers the country to the city, but she shows us both in these stories, and, though the country usually wins out, she does indicate some positive aspects of town life. The high school and college boys and girls in these stories are in towns, and it is there that they finally discover their kin. Education is important to these young people, and it must be obtained in academies in town. When that education is achieved and family ties are renewed, a happy ending is inevitable.

In the "school stories" we also meet the gently didactic Montgomery. She is not overtly preachy, but shows that a good deed is a pleasant thing, often beneficial in more ways than might be suspected. She wants her readers to know that the "right thing to do," however difficult, is ultimately rewarding, always for conscience's sake and sometimes in other ways as well.

Montgomery gives us a great range of characters within the "orphan" theme. She writes of rich people: pleasant or snobbish or nasty, born to money or nouveau riche. She writes of social climbers and of those to whom "society" matters not a whit. She writes of all ages: Charlotte of "Charlotte's Quest" is the youngest, Miss Sally the oldest. She writes of poor people: good and bad, generous and parsimonious, loving and unloving, gentle guardians and stern taskmasters. Wealth is no guarantee of happiness; poverty is not necessarily bad. The most important need in the lives of these characters is a warm and loving home, and each of them finds one.

REA WILMSHURST

Charlotte's

Quest

Sometime she had been here before. Not in a dream, but really and her mother had been with her.

HARLOTTE had made up her mind to see the Witch Penny about it. Perhaps God didn't think she ought to be unhappy, in a home of jolly, noisy, rollicking cousins (Charlotte hated noise and rollicking with all the power of her being); where she was continually being pounced on and petted and kissed (Charlotte detested pouncing and petting and kissing); where Aunt Florence or Cousin Edith or Mrs. Barrett, the grandmother of the gang, was always trying to dress her up like a doll (Charlotte hated to be dressed up); and where she was never alone or lonely for a moment (Charlotte loved and longed to be alone – well, not exactly lonely, because Charlotte was never lonely when she was alone). Yes, it was quite likely, Charlotte told herself, on considered reflection, that God couldn't believe that she was unhappy. So there remained only Witch Penny. Charlotte had an idea that witches were kittle cattle to have dealings with and that the thing was not altogether lawful. But she wanted a mother so desperately that she would have gone to any lengths to get one.

It was Jim who had told her about the Witch Penny very soon after she had come to live with Aunt Florence.

"The Witch Penny is going to fly to a witches' meeting tonight with her old black cat perched behind her," he told her one windy autumn evening. And then he went on with a fascinating rigmarole about riding on a broomstick over houses and hills. Jim did not mean to be fascinating. He was merely trying to frighten Charlotte "out of her skin." But Charlotte was not easily frightened and remained in her skin. She found his yarns thrilling, especially the part about flying on a broomstick, although she would have preferred to fly on a swallow's back. Why couldn't you, if you were a witch? If you could turn yourself into a grey cat, as Jim said Witch Penny could, why couldn't you turn yourself into something small enough to ride a swallow? Just think of swooping through the air. Charlotte quivered with ecstasy.

Charlotte wanted a mother terribly. She knew that the thing was quite possible. Before father had gone away and just before she had come to Aunt Florence's, Nita Gresham had got a new mother. Charlotte heard about it in school. If Nita, why not she? A mother who would take you in her arms and tell you stories. To whom you would belong. It seemed a terrible thing to Charlotte that she didn't belong anywhere or to anybody. Not even to Father. How could you belong to a father who looked upon you merely as a hindrance to mountain climbing? Charlotte knew perfectly well that was how her father regarded her, although neither he nor anyone else had ever told her so. You couldn't fool Charlotte in all things. She might fall for a silly story about witches and broomsticks, but in some respects she had a terrible wisdom.

Next to a mother she wanted a quiet place where she could be alone when she wanted to be; to listen to the wind telling strange tales, or hold the big spotted shell that murmured of the sea to her ear, or talk to the roses in the garden. Or just sit still and think and say nothing. If you were quiet at Aunt Florence's, someone was sure to ask what was the matter with you. And if your visitation of silence was prolonged they said you were sulky. It had not been quite so bad when she had lived at home, a kind of home, with Father and old Mrs. Beckwith. At least they left her alone. If you couldn't be loved, the next best thing was to be let alone. At Aunt Florence's she was never let alone and she knew quite well they didn't love her. They kissed and petted and teased her just because it was one of their customs. Jim thought her a ninny. Edith and Susette thought her a dumb-bell. Mrs. Barrett thought she was "queer," and Aunt Florence couldn't make her pretty.

"Goodness, child, are you all corners?" she would exclaim impatiently when Charlotte's dress wouldn't hang right. Aunt Florence hadn't any use for anyone with too many corners. And nothing else about Charlotte pleased her. She was too dark in a fair clan, her eyes were too big and grey, her eyebrows too bushy and her skin too sallow. "I don't know where she gets such a complexion," Aunt Florence mourned.

"Don't you? I do," said Mrs. Barrett very significantly. "She's the living image of You-Know-Who."

"I never saw her," said Aunt Florence, "but if Charlotte looks like her, I don't wonder Edward isn't fond of her."

So her father wasn't fond of her. Charlotte sighed. She had always suspected it, but it was a little bitter to be sure of it. She had always thought it was because he couldn't be fond of anything but mountain climbing. Now it seemed there was a mysterious You-Know-Who in the business.

Charlotte knew she didn't look like her mother. There was no picture of her mother that Charlotte had even seen, but she knew she had been small and fair and golden. Charlotte wished she looked like her mother. She couldn't remember her mother, that is, not exactly. She could only remember a dream she had had about her, a beautiful dream in which she was in such a beautiful place. And Mother was there with her. Charlotte had never forgotten it – she was always looking for it. An old house fronting seaward, ships going up and down. Spruce woods and misty hills, cold salt air from the water, rest, quiet, silence. And the most beautiful china lady, with blue shoes and a gilt sash and a red rose in her golden china hair, sitting on a shelf.

Mother had been there with her. Charlotte was quite sure of that, though everything else was a little dim, as dreams are. Charlotte always had a queer feeling that if she could find that place she would find Mother again. But it was not likely that even Witch Penny could help her to a place in a dream.

Charlotte determined to slip away on the afternoon they were getting ready for the party. They were always having parties. "Let us eat, drink and be merry," was the motto of the Laurences. Charlotte hated parties and she knew she would hate this more than most because they were going to have tableaux and Charlotte was to take part in one and wear a silly tinsel crown. Somehow, she hated the thought of that tinsel crown venomously.

In the customary scurry and bustle she hoped to get away unseen, but Mrs. Barrett spied her and asked her where she was going.

"I am going hunting for happiness," said Charlotte gravely and simply. The truth had to be told.

Mrs. Barrett stared at her.

"I don't know who you get your peculiar notions from. Any child but you would be keen to help get ready for a party. Look at your cousins – what a delightful time they're having."

Probably they were. Everybody was rushing wildly around, moving and dragging furniture about. But they were always doing that. Nothing ever remained in the same place longer than a week. Just as you got used to a thing being in a certain place, Aunt Florence or Susette took a notion it would look better somewhere else; and after much noisy, good-natured argument, there it went. And a party always gave such a grand excuse for moving everything.

Charlotte did not reply to Mrs. Barrett, which was another of her unsatisfactory habits. She simply opened the door, went out and shut it softly behind her. It was hard to shut it softly because, like every other door in the house, it seemed determined to bang shut. But Charlotte managed it.

She stood for a moment in the front porch, drawing a breath of relief. Behind her was noise and commotion. Edith and Susette were wrangling in the hall. The radio was going full blare in the library, Jim was banging on the piano to make the fat dog howl – and the dog was howling. Charlotte put her fingers in her ears and ran down the walk. Over her was a grey, quiet autumn sky, and before her a grey, quiet road. Charlotte suddenly felt as light of being as if she really had been turned into a swallow. She was out, she was alone and she was going to find a mother.

THE WITCH PENNY'S HOUSE was a little grey one nestling against the steep hill that rose from the pond about half a mile west of the small town. The gate hung slackly on its hinges. The house itself was shabby and old, with sunken window sills and a much-patched roof. Charlotte reflected that being a witch didn't seem to be a very profitable business.

For a moment Charlotte hesitated. She was not a timid child, but she did feel a little frightened. Then she thought of Mrs. Barrett rocking fiercely in her rocker and forever talking in her high, cheerful voice. "Mother is always so bright," Aunt Florence always said. Charlotte shuddered. No witch could be worse. She knocked resolutely on the door.

A thumping sound inside ceased. Had she interrupted Witch Penny in the weaving of a spell? . . . and footsteps seemed to be coming down a stair. Then the door opened and Witch Penny appeared. Charlotte took her all in with one of her straight, deliberate looks.

She was grey as an owl, with a broad rosy face and tiny black eyes surrounded by cushions of fat. Charlotte thought she looked too jolly for a witch. But no doubt there were all kinds. Certainly the big black cat with fiery golden eyes that sat behind her on the lower step of the stair looked his reputed part.

"Now who may ye be and what may ye be wanting with me?" said Witch Penny a bit gruffly.

Charlotte never wasted breath, words or time. "I am Charlotte Laurence and I have come to ask you to find me a mother – that is, if you really are a witch. Are you?"

Witch Penny's look suddenly changed. It grew secretive and mysterious.

"Whist, child," she whispered. "Don't be talking of witches in the open daylight like this. Little ye know what might happen."

"But are you?" persisted Charlotte. If Witch Penny wasn't a witch, she wasn't going to bother with her.

"To be sure, I am. But come in, come in. Finding a mother ain't something to be done on the durestep. Better come right upstairs. I'm weaving a tablecloth for the fairies up there. All the witches in the countryside promised to do one apiece for them. The poor liddle shiftless craturs left all their tablecloths out in the frost last Tuesday night, and 'twas their ruination. But I've got far behind me comrades and mustn't be losing any more time. Ye'll excuse me if I kape on with me work while ye're telling me your troubles. It's the quane's own cloth I'm weaving, and it's looking sour enough her majesty will be if it's not finished on time."

Charlotte thought that Witch Penny's old loom looked very big and clumsy for the weaving of fairy tablecloths, and the web in it seemed strangely like rather coarse grey flannel. But no doubt witches had their own way of blinding the eyes of ordinary mortals. When Witch Penny finished it, she would weave a spell over it and it would become a thing of gossamer light and loveliness.

Witch Penny resumed her work and Charlotte sat down on a stool beside her. They were on a little landing above the stairs, with one low, cobwebby window and a stained ceiling with bunches of dried tansy and yarrow hanging from it. The cat had followed them up and sat on the top step, staring at Charlotte. Its eyes shone uncannily through the dusk of the staircase.

"Now, out with your story," said Witch Penny. "Ye're wanting a mother, ye tell me, and ye're Charlotte Laurence. Ye'll be having Edward Laurence for your father, I'm thinking?"

"Yes. But he's gone west to climb mountains," explained Charlotte. "He's always wanted to, but Mother died when I was three, and as long as I was small he couldn't. I'm eight now, so he's gone."

"And left ye with your Uncle Tom and your Aunt Florence. Oh, I've heard all about it. Your Aunt Florence's cat was after telling mine the whole story at the last dance we had. Your Aunt Florence do be too grand for the likes of us, but it's little she thinks where her cat do be going. Ye don't look like the Laurences – ye haven't got your father's laughing mouth – ye've got a proud mouth like your old Grandmother Jasper. Did ye ever see her?"

Charlotte shook her head. She knew nothing of her Grandmother Jasper beyond the fact of her existence, but all at once she knew who You-Know-Who was.

"No, it ain't likely ye would. She was real mad at your mother for marrying Ned Laurence. I've heard she never would forgive her, never would set foot in her house. But ye have her mouth. And what black hair ye've got. And what big eyes. And what little ears. And ye have a mole on your neck. 'Tis the witch's mark. Come now, child dear, wouldn't ye like to be made a witch? 'Tis a far easier job than the one ye've set me. Think av the fun av riding on the broomstick."

Charlotte thought of it. Flying over the steeples and dark spruces at night. "I think I'm too young to be a witch," she said.

Witch Penny's eyes twinkled.

"Sure, child dear, 'tis the young witches that do be having the most power. Mind ye, everybody can't be a witch. We're that exclusive ye'd never belave. But I'll not press ye. And ye want me to find you a mother?"

"If you please. Nita Gresham got a new mother. So why can't I?"

"Well, the real mothers are hard to come by. All the same, mebbe it can be managed. It's lucky ye've come in the right time of the moon. I couldn't have done a thing for ye next wake. And mind ye, child dear, I'm not after promising anything for sartin. But there's a chanct, there's a chanct . . . seeing as ye've got your grand-mother's mouth. If ye'd looked like your father, it wouldn't be Witch Penny as'd help ye to a mother. I'd no use for him."

Witch Penny chuckled. "What kind of a mother do ye be wanting?"

"A quiet mother who doesn't laugh too much or ask too many questions."

Witch Penny shook her head.

"A rare kind. It'll take some conniving. Here . . ." Witch Penny dropped her shuttle, leaned forward and extract-ed from a box beside the loom a handful of raisins . . . "stow these away in your liddle inside while I do a bit av thinking."

Charlotte ate her raisins with a relish while Witch Penny wove slowly and thoughtfully. She did not speak until Charlotte had finished the last raisin.

"It come into me mind," said Witch Penny, "that if ye

go up the long hill . . . and down it . . . then turn yourself about three times, nather more nor less, ye'll find a road that goes west. Folly your nose along it till ye come to a gate with a liddle lane that leads down to the harbour shore. Turn yourself about three times more . . . if ye forget that part of it, ye may look till your eyes fall out of your head, but niver a mother ye'll see. Then go down the lane to a stone house with a red door in it like a cat's tongue. Knock three times on the door. If there's a mother in the world for ye, ye'll find her there. That's all I can be doing for ye."

Charlotte got up briskly.

"Thank you very much. It sounds like a good long walk, so I ought to start. What am I to pay you for this?"

Witch Penny chuckled again. Something seemed to amuse her greatly.

"How much have ye got?" she asked.

"A dollar."

"How'd ye come by it?"

Charlotte thought witches were rather impertinent. However, if you dealt with them . . .

"Mrs. Beckwith gave it to me before she went away."

"And how come ye didn't spend it for swaties and ice cream?"

"I like to feel I've something to fall back on," said Charlotte gravely.

Witch Penny chuckled for the third time.

"Says your grandmother. Oh, ye're Laurence be name but it goes no daper. Kape your liddle bit av a dollar. Ye've got a mole on your neck. We can't charge folks as have moles anything. It's clane against our rules. Now run along or it'll be getting too late."

"I'm very much obliged to you," said Charlotte, putting her money back in her pocket and offering her thin brown hand.

"Ye do be a mannerly child at that," said Witch Penny.

Witch Penny stood on her sunken doorstep and watched the little, erect figure out of sight.

"Sure, and I do be wondering if I've done right. But she'd never fit in up at the Laurences with their clatter. And once the old leddy lays eyes on her!"

Charlotte had disappeared around the bend in the road. Then Witch Penny said a queer thing for a witch. She said: "God bless the liddle cratur."

CHARLOTTE TRAMPED sturdily on, adventurous and expectant. The sky grew greyer and the wind colder as she climbed the long hill. From the top she caught an unexpected, breath-taking view of a great grey harbour with white-capped racing waves. And beyond its sandy bar something greater and greyer still which she knew must be the sea. Charlotte stood for a few minutes in an ecstasy. She had never seen the harbour before, although she had known it was not far away. And yet, had she not? Charlotte felt bewildered. Her dream came back to her. She had seen this harbour in her dream, with the big waves racing to the shore and the black crows sitting on the fences of the fields and a white bird flying against the dark sky.

Charlotte went down the hill and gravely turned herself about three times. A wind that smelt of the sea came blowing down a road to the left. This must be what Witch Penny meant by following her nose. And sure enough, after Charlotte had walked along the road for a little while, there was the gate and a grassy, deep-rutted lane leading along the side of a gentle hill that sloped to the harbour.

Again Charlotte turned herself around. If there were no mother at the end of this quest, it should not be for any failure to perform Witch Penny's ritual scrupulously.

Halfway along the hill she came to the house, the grey stone house with the door like a cat's tongue, a house so grey and old that it seemed a part of the hill. It had a dignified, reposeful look as if it feared not what wind or rain could do to it.

Charlotte found her legs trembling under her. She had come to journey's end; and was there a mother in that house for her? Witch Penny hadn't seemed at all sure, she had only said there was a chance. It was beginning to rain, the harbour was dim and misty, it would soon be dark. Charlotte shivered, took her courage in both hands and knocked at the red door.

There was no answer. Charlotte waited awhile and then went around the house to the kitchen door – it was red, too – and knocked again.

The door opened. Charlotte felt a quick pang of disappointment. This was no mother: she was far too old for a mother, this tall, thin woman with a fine old face that might have been a man's and clear grey eyes with black bushy brows under frosty hair. Charlotte had never seen her before yet she had a queer feeling that the face was quite familiar to her.

"Who are you?" said the old woman, neither kindly nor unkindly . . . just in a simple, direct fashion to which Charlotte found it quite easy to respond.

"I am Charlotte Laurence. I went to Witch Penny to see if she could find me a mother and she told me to come here."

The old woman stood still for what seemed to Charlotte a very long moment. Then she stepped back and said, "Come in."

Charlotte looked around the little, white-washed kitchen. There was, to her further disappointment, no one in it, but she liked it. On the floor there was a big, dark-red, hooked rug, with three black cats in it. The cats had yellow wool eyes that were quite bright and catty in spite of the fact that they had evidently been walked over a good many years. There was a great stove with front doors that slid so far back that it was as good as a fireplace. There was a low wide window looking out on the harbour. There was a table with a red-and-white checkered cloth on it and a platterful of something that smelt very good to Charlotte after her long walk.

"I was just sitting down to supper," said the old woman. "I had a feeling that I was going to have company so I cooked a bit extra. Take off your cap and coat and sit in."

Charlotte silently did as she was told. The old woman sat down, said grace . . . Charlotte liked that . . . and gave Charlotte a plentiful helping of crisp bacon and pancakes with maple syrup poured over them. Charlotte devoted herself to the business of eating. She had never been so hungry in her life before and she had never eaten anything that tasted so good as the bacon and pancakes. It was now raining and blowing quite wildly but the stove was glowing clear red in the dusk and the peace and cosiness of the old kitchen was in delightful contrast to the storm outside. And just to eat supper in silence, not having to talk or laugh unless you really wanted to, was so heavenly. Charlotte thought of the noisy meals at Aunt Florence's where everybody talked and laughed incessantly . . . Aunt Florence liked "cheerful meals."

OF COURSE, as yet there was no mother. But one must have patience. It was easy to be patient here. Charlotte found herself liking the house . . . feeling at home in it. It was not strange to her . . . and the old woman was not strange. Charlotte wondered where she had seen eyes like that before, many times before. And she loved the house. She wanted to see the hidden things in it – not its furniture or its carpets, but the letters in old boxes upstairs, and faded photos and clothes in old trunks. It seemed as if they belonged to her. She sighed in pure happiness. The old woman did not ask her why she sighed. That, too, was heavenly.

When the meal was over, the old woman – after all Charlotte was beginning to think she wasn't so very old, it was just her white hair made you think so – put Charlotte in a chair by the stove where she could toast her feet on the warm hearth, and washed the dishes. Her shadow darted in all directions over the kitchen walls and ceiling and sometimes looked more like a witch than Witch Penny. But this woman was not a witch. Somehow, Charlotte felt no qualms on that score.

When the old woman had put her dishes away in a little corner cupboard with glass doors and shelves trimmed with white, scalloped lace paper, she lighted a lamp, got out her knitting and sat down by the table.

"You're Charlotte Laurence. And your father, I suppose, was Edward Laurence."

Charlotte nodded.

"Where is he?"

"He has gone to climb mountains in British Columbia and he sent me to stay with Aunt Florence while he was away."

"How long is he going to be away?"

"Years," said Charlotte indifferently.

The old woman knitted two rounds of her stocking before she said anything else.

"Do you like it at your Aunt Florence's?"

"No. It's too noisy and affectionate," said Charlotte gravely.

The old woman laid down her knitting and stared at

her. There was a queer expression on her face, she might almost have been going to laugh. Her thick black eyebrows twitched.

"Does your aunt know where you are?"

Charlotte shook her head.

"And don't you think she'll be worried? I don't think you can get back tonight in this storm."

"She's always worried over something," said Charlotte, as if it didn't matter a great deal. Nobody had ever worried much about her. And she was very well satisfied with where she was. She had never been in a place or in such company that suited her so well. Only, as yet, no mother. But it was quiet and peaceful and warm. The wood snapped and crackled in the stove. The rain spattered on the window panes. The wind growled and snarled because it could not get into the sturdy house.

"We're neither of us much for talking, it seems," said the old woman.

"No, but I think we are entertaining each other very well," said Charlotte.

This time the old woman did really laugh.

"I've had some such thought myself," she said.

It was quite a long while, a long, delightful while, after that Charlotte found herself nodding. And the downtrodden black cats had begun to trot around the rug.

"You're half asleep. You'd be better in bed. Are you afraid to sleep alone?"

Afraid? Charlotte loved to sleep alone. And she never could at Aunt Florence's. She did not even have a steady room, always being passed about from one to the other. Now Mrs. Barrett who snored, now Jenny who kicked, now Edith or Susette who fussed over her.

"I like sleeping alone," said Charlotte.

The old woman filled a little blue rubber bag with hot water from the puffing kettle and lighted a candle in a little blue china candlestick. She took Charlotte through a large room, with only a little plain furniture in it. You could move around in it without knocking something over. It was not cluttered up with over-stuffed divans or gilt fandangos, but full of dancing, inviting shadows from the candle. Charlotte felt sure that this room was never in a hurry. Then they went up a staircase of shining black steps and into a bedroom where there was a bed with a pink flounced spread. The old woman set the candle on the bureau, turned back the bedclothes and put the blue bottle in the bed.

"I hope you'll be warm and have a good night," she said. There was something in her face that was very kind. Charlotte felt emboldened to ask a question.

"Would you mind telling me if I'm likely to find a mother here?"

"We'll see about that in the morning," said the old woman as she went out and shut the brown door with the big brass latch.

Charlotte looked about the room. She loved it: and it was a room that was used to being loved. Charlotte was quite sure of that. It had a hooked rug on the floor with great soft plushy roses and ferns in it, flowered chintz curtains at the window, and a blue-and-white pitcher and wash basin. And everything in it felt related to her.

On the wall over the table was the picture of a little girl in an old-fashioned dress . . . a little girl not much older than Charlotte. She looked very sweet and young and innocent with the little puffs at her shoulders and the big bow of ribbon in her hair. Charlotte felt acquainted with her.

And then she saw it, the china lady with the blue shoes and the gilt sash and the unfaded red rose in her golden hair, sitting on the little frilled shelf in the corner . . . the china lady of her dream. There could be no mistake about it. Sometime she had been here before . . . not in a dream but really. And her mother had been with her.

Charlotte got into bed, feeling perfectly at home. When she wakened in the morning to see sunshine raining all over her bed, the old woman was bending over her.

"Is that Mother's picture?" were the first words Charlotte said.

"Yes. This used to be her room. This is not the first time you have been in it. Have you any recollection of it, child?"

"Yes. I thought it was a dream until last night. And Mother was here with me, wasn't she?"

"Yes. I am your grandmother, Elizabeth Jasper. Your mother married a man I'd no use for. People will tell you I never forgave her. That was nonsense. It's true I never went to see her. I wouldn't cross the threshold of Ned Laurence's house. But she came here to see me and brought you. We made up for all our coolness. She died soon afterwards. I couldn't bring myself to have anything to do with your father. I see I was wrong. I shouldn't have left him to bring you up to hate me."

"But he didn't. He just never said anything about you," said Charlotte, sitting up in bed. She knew now that no new mother was to be found, but somehow she did not feel disappointed. She seemed so close to her own mother. The room, the house, was full of her.

"Judith Penny sent you here to find a mother. She isn't called a witch for nothing, that one. I'm sorry I haven't got a mother for you. Do you think a grandmother would do?"

Charlotte knew all at once where she had seen Grandmother Jasper's eyes so often. In her looking glass. She was suddenly so happy that it seemed to her she must burst with her happiness.

"Can I live here with you?" she whispered. Grandmother Jasper nodded.

"I telephoned your aunt last night after you went to bed and told her where you were. I told her you might stay here quite likely. She didn't seem to mind."

"Oh, she wouldn't. Grandmother, it's so quiet here!"

Grandmother nodded.

"We're alike in more than our looks, child. What a turn you gave me when I opened the door last night. I thought I was seeing the ghost of the child I was fifty years ago."

"Grandmother," said Charlotte curiously, "is Witch Penny really a witch?"

"If she isn't, she ought to be," said Grandmother Jasper.

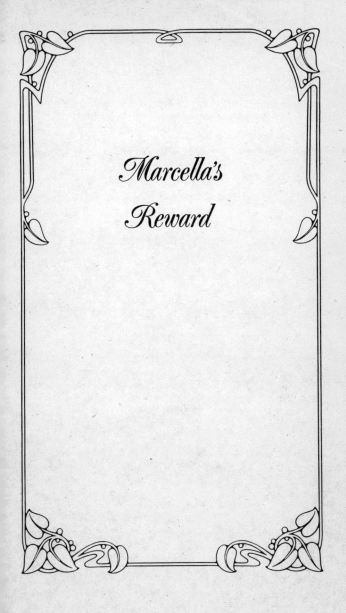

Marcella's
Reward

R. CLARK shook his head gravely. "She is not improving as fast as I should like to see," he said. "In fact – er – she seems to have gone backward the past week. You must send her to the country, Miss Langley. The heat here is too trying for her."

Dr. Clark might as well have said, "You must send her to the moon" – or so Marcella thought bitterly. Despair filled her heart as she looked at Patty's white face and transparent hands and listened to the doctor's coolly professional advice. Patty's illness had already swept away the scant savings of three years. Marcella had nothing left with which to do anything more for her.

She did not make any answer to the doctor – she could not. Besides, what could she say, with Patty's big blue eyes, bigger and bluer than ever in her thin face, looking at her so wistfully? She dared not say it was impossible. But Aunt Emma had no such scruples. With a great clatter and racket, that lady fell upon the dishes that held Patty's almost untasted dinner and whisked them away while her tongue kept time to her jerky movements.

"Goodness me, doctor, do you think you're talking to millionaires? Where do you suppose the money is to come from to send Patty to the country? *I* can't afford it, that is certain. I think I do pretty well to give Marcella and Patty their board free, and I have to work my fingers to the bone to do *that*. It's all nonsense about Patty, anyhow. What she ought to do is to make an effort to get better. She doesn't – she just mopes and pines. She won't eat a thing I cook for her. How can anyone expect to get better if she doesn't eat?"

Aunt Emma glared at the doctor as if she were triumphantly sure that she had propounded an unanswerable question. A dull red flush rose to Marcella's face.

"Oh, Aunt Emma, I *can't* eat!" said Patty wearily. "It isn't because I won't – indeed, I can't."

"Humph! I suppose my cooking isn't fancy enough for you – that's the trouble. Well, I haven't the time to put any frills on it. I think I do pretty well to wait on you at all with all that work piling up before me. But some people imagine that they were born to be waited on."

Aunt Emma whirled the last dish from the table and left the room, slamming the door behind her.

The doctor shrugged his shoulders. He had become used to Miss Gibson's tirades during Patty's illness. But Marcella had never got used to them – never, in all the three years she had lived with her aunt. They flicked on the raw as keenly as ever. This morning it seemed unbearable. It took every atom of Marcella's self-control to keep her from voicing her resentful thoughts. It was only for Patty's sake that she was able to restrain herself. It was only for Patty's sake, too, that she did not, as soon as the doctor had gone, give way to tears. Instead, she smiled bravely into the little sister's eyes.

"Let me brush your hair now, dear, and bathe your face."

"Have you time?" said Patty anxiously.

"Yes, I think so."

Patty gave a sigh of content.

"I'm so glad! Aunt Emma always hurts me when she brushes my hair – she is in such a hurry. You're so gentle, Marcella, you don't make my head ache at all. But oh! I'm so tired of being sick. I wish I could get well faster. Marcy, do you think I can be sent to the country?"

"I – I don't know, dear. I'll see if I can think of any way to manage it," said Marcella, striving to speak hopefully.

Patty drew a long breath.

"Oh, Marcy, it would be lovely to see the green fields again, and the woods and brooks, as we did that summer we spent in the country before Father died. I wish we could live in the country always. I'm sure I would soon get better if I could go – if it was only for a little while. It's so hot here – and the factory makes such a noise – my head seems to go round and round all the time. And Aunt Emma scolds so."

"You mustn't mind Aunt Emma, dear," said Marcella. "You know she doesn't really mean it – it is just a habit she has got into. She was really very good to you when you were so sick. She sat up night after night with you, and made me go to bed. There now, dearie, you're fresh and sweet, and I must hurry to the store, or I'll be late. Try and have a little nap, and I'll bring you home some oranges tonight."

Marcella dropped a kiss on Patty's cheek, put on her hat and went out. As soon as she left the house, she quickened her steps almost to a run. She feared she would be late, and that meant a ten-cent fine. Ten cents loomed as large as ten dollars now to Marcella's eyes when every dime meant so much. But fast as she went, her distracted thoughts went faster. She could not send Patty to the country. There was no way, think, plan, worry as she might. And if she could not! Marcella remembered Patty's face and the doctor's look, and her heart sank like lead. Patty was growing weaker every day instead of stronger, and the weather was getting hotter. Oh, if Patty were to – to – but Marcella could not complete the sentence even in thought.

If they were not so desperately poor! Marcella's bitterness overflowed her soul at the thought. Everywhere around her were evidences of wealth – wealth often lavishly and foolishly spent – and she could not get money enough anywhere to save her sister's life! She almost felt that she hated all those smiling, well-dressed people who thronged the streets. By the time she reached the store, poor Marcella's heart was seething with misery and resentment.

Three years before, when Marcella had been sixteen and Patty nine, their parents had died, leaving them absolutely alone in the world except for their father's half-sister, Miss Gibson, who lived in Canning and earned her livelihood washing and mending for the hands employed in the big factory nearby. She had grudgingly offered the girls a home, which Marcella had accepted because she must. She obtained a position in one of the Canning stores at three dollars a week, out of which she contrived to dress herself and Patty and send the latter to school. Her life for three years was one of absolute drudgery, yet until now she had never lost courage, but had struggled bravely on, hoping for better times in the future when she should get promotion and Patty would be old enough to teach school.

But now Marcella's courage and hopefulness had gone out like a spent candle. She was late at the store, and that meant a fine; her head ached, and her feet felt like lead as she climbed the stairs to her department – a hot, dark, stuffy corner behind the shirtwaist counter. It was warm and close at any time, but today it was stifling, and there was already a crowd of customers, for it was the day of a bargain sale. The heat and noise and chatter got on Marcella's tortured nerves. She felt that she wanted to scream, but instead she turned calmly to a waiting customer – a big, handsome, richly dressed woman. Marcella noted with an ever-increasing bitterness that the woman wore a lace collar the price of which would have kept Patty in the country for a year.

She was Mrs. Liddell – Marcella knew her by sight – and she was in a very bad temper because she had been kept waiting. For the next half hour she badgered and worried Marcella to the point of distraction. Nothing suited her. Pile after pile, box after box, of shirtwaists did Marcella take down for her, only to have them flung aside with sarcastic remarks. Mrs. Liddell seemed to hold Marcella responsible for the lack of waists that suited her; her tongue grew sharper and sharper and her comments more trying. Then she mislaid her purse, and was disagreeable about that until it turned up.

Marcella shut her lips so tightly that they turned white to keep back the impatient retort that rose momentarily to her lips. The insolence of some customers was always trying to the sensitive, high-spirited girl, but today it seemed unbearable. Her head throbbed fiercely with the pain of the ever-increasing ache, and – what was the lady on her right saying to a friend?

"Yes, she had typhoid, you know – a very bad form. She rallied from it, but she was so exhausted that she couldn't really recover, and the doctor said –"

"Really," interrupted Mrs. Liddell's sharp voice, "may I ask you to attend to me, if you please? No doubt gossip may be very interesting to you, but I am accustomed to having a clerk pay *some* small attention to my requirements. If you cannot attend to your business, I shall go to the floor walker and ask him to direct me to somebody who can. The laziness and disobligingness of the girls in this store is really getting beyond endurance."

A passionate answer was on the point of Marcella's tongue. All her bitterness and suffering and resentment flashed into her face and eyes. For one moment she was determined to speak out, to repay Mrs. Liddell's insolence in kind. A retort was ready to her hand. Everyone knew that Mrs. Liddell, before her marriage to a wealthy man, had been a working girl. What could be easier than to say contemptuously: "You should be a judge of a clerk's courtesy and ability, madam. You were a shop girl yourself once"?

But if she said it, what would follow? Prompt and instant dismissal. And Patty? The thought of the little sister quelled the storm in Marcella's soul. For Patty's sake she must control her temper – and she did. With an effort that left her white and tremulous she crushed back the hot words and said quietly: "I beg your pardon, Mrs. Liddell. I did not mean to be inattentive. Let me show you some of our new lingerie waists, I think you will like them."

But Mrs. Liddell did not like the new lingerie waists which Marcella brought to her in her trembling hands. For another half hour she examined and found fault and sneered. Then she swept away with the scornful remark that she didn't see a thing there that was fit to wear, and she would go to Markwell Bros. and see if they had anything worth looking at.

When she had gone, Marcella leaned against the counter, pale and exhausted. She must have a breathing spell. Oh, how her head ached! How hot and stifling and horrible everything was! She longed for the country herself. Oh, if she and Patty could only go away to some place where there were green clover meadows and cool breezes and great hills where the air was sweet and pure!

During all this time a middle-aged woman had been sitting on a stool beside the bargain counter. When a clerk asked her if she wished to be waited on, she said, "No, I'm just waiting here for a friend who promised to meet me."

She was tall and gaunt and grey haired. She had square jaws and cold grey eyes and an aggressive nose, but there was something attractive in her plain face, a mingling of common sense and kindliness. She watched Marcella and Mrs. Liddell closely and lost nothing of all that was said and done on both sides. Now and then she smiled grimly and nodded.

When Mrs. Liddell had gone, she rose and leaned over the counter. Marcella opened her burning eyes and pulled herself wearily together.

"What can I do for you?" she said.

"Nothing. I ain't looking for to have anything done for me. You need to have something done for you, I guess, by the looks of you. You seem dead beat out. Aren't you awful tired? I've been listening to that woman jawing you till I felt like rising up and giving her a large and whole-some piece of my mind. I don't know how you kept your patience with her, but I can tell you I admired you for it, and I made up my mind I'd tell you so."

The kindness and sympathy in her tone broke Marcella down. Tears rushed to her eyes. She bowed her head on her hands and said sobbingly, "Oh, I *am* tired! But it's not that. I'm – I'm in such trouble."

"I knew you were," said the other, with a nod of her head. "I could tell that right off by your face. Do you know what I said to myself? I said, 'That girl has got somebody at home awful sick.' *That's* what I said. Was I right?"

"Yes, indeed you were," said Marcella.

"I knew it" – another triumphant nod. "Now, you just tell me all about it. It'll do you good to talk it over with somebody. Here, I'll pretend I'm looking at shirtwaists, so that floor walker won't be coming down on you, and I'll be as hard to please as that other woman was, so's you can take your time. Who's sick – and what's the matter?"

Marcella told the whole story, choking back her sobs and forcing herself to speak calmly, having the fear of the floor walker before her eyes.

"And I can't afford to send Patty to the country – I *can't* – and I know she won't get better if she doesn't go," she concluded.

"Dear, dear, but that's too bad! Something must be

done. Let me see – let *me* put on my thinking cap. What is your name?"

"Marcella Langley."

The older woman dropped the lingerie waist she was pretending to examine and stared at Marcella.

"You don't say! Look here, what was your mother's name before she was married?"

"Mary Carvell."

"Well, I *have* heard of coincidences, but this beats all! Mary Carvell! Well, did you ever hear your mother speak of a girl friend of hers called Josephine Draper?"

"I should think I did! You don't mean –"

"I *do* mean it. I'm Josephine Draper. Your mother and I went to school together, and we were as much as sisters to each other until she got married. Then she went away, and after a few years I lost trace of her. I didn't even know she was dead. Poor Mary! Well, *my* duty is plain – that's one comfort – my duty and my pleasure, too. Your sister is coming out to Dalesboro to stay with me. Yes, and you are too, for the whole summer. You needn't say you're not, because you *are*. I've said so. There's room at Fir Cottage for you both. Yes, Fir Cottage – I guess you've heard your mother speak of *that*. There's her old room out there that we always slept in when she came to stay all night with me. It's all ready for you. What's that? You can't afford to lose your place here? Bless your heart, child, you won't lose it! The owner of this store is my nephew, and he'll do considerable to oblige me, as well he might, seeing as I brought him up. To think that Mary Carvell's daughter has been in his store for three years, and me never suspecting it! And I might never have found you out at all if you hadn't been so patient with that woman. If you'd sassed her back, I'd have thought she deserved it and wouldn't have blamed you a mite, but I wouldn't have bothered coming to talk to you either. Well, well, well! Poor child, don't cry. You just pick up and go home. I'll make it all right with Tom. You're pretty near played out yourself, I can see that. But a summer in Fir Cottage, with plenty of cream and eggs and *my* cookery, will soon make another girl of you. Don't you dare to *thank* me. It's a privilege to be able to do something for Mary Carvell's girls. I just loved Mary."

The upshot of the whole matter was that Marcella and Patty went, two days later, to Dalesboro, where Miss Draper gave them a hearty welcome to Fir Cottage – a quaint, delightful little house circled by big Scotch firs and overgrown with vines. Never were such delightful weeks as those that followed. Patty came rapidly back to health and strength. As for Marcella, Miss Draper's prophecy was also fulfilled; she soon looked and felt like another girl. The dismal years of drudgery behind her were forgotten like a dream, and she lived wholly in the beautiful present, in the walks and drives, the flowers and grass slopes, and in the pleasant household duties which she shared with Miss Draper.

"I love housework," she exclaimed one September day. "I don't like the thought of going back to the store a bit."

"Well, you're not going back," calmly said Miss Draper, who had a habit of arranging other people's business for them that might have been disconcerting had it not been for her keen insight and hearty good sense. "You're going to stay here with me – you and Patty. I don't propose to die of lonesomeness losing you, and I need somebody to help me about the house. I've thought it all out. You are to call me Aunt Josephine, and Patty is to go to school. I had this scheme in mind from the first, but I thought I'd wait to see how we got along living in the same house, and how you liked it here, before I spoke out. No, you needn't thank me this time either. I'm doing this every bit as much for my sake as yours. Well, that's all settled. Patty won't object, bless her rosy cheeks!"

"Oh!" said Marcella, with eyes shining through her tears. "I'm so happy, dear Miss Draper – I mean Aunt Josephine. I'll love to stay here – and I *will* thank you."

"Fudge!" remarked Miss Draper, who felt uncomfortably near crying herself. "You might go out and pick a basket of Golden Gems. I want to make some jelly for Patty."

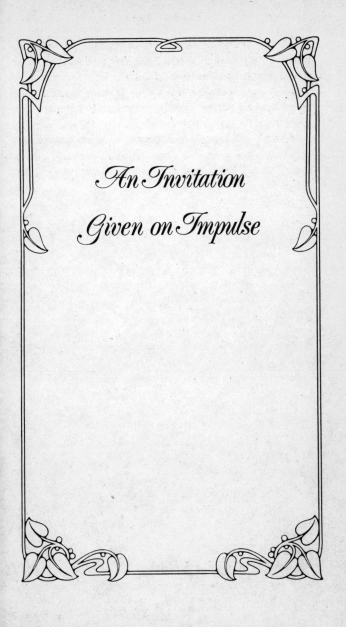

An Invitation

Given on Impulse

T WAS A gloomy Saturday morning. The trees in the Oaklawn grounds were tossing wildly in the gusts of wind, and sodden brown leaves were blown up against the windows of the library, where a score of girls were waiting for the principal to bring the mail in.

The big room echoed with the pleasant sound of girlish voices and low laughter, for in a fortnight school would close for the holidays, and they were all talking about their plans and anticipations.

Only Ruth Mannering was, as usual, sitting by herself near one of the windows, looking out on the misty lawn. She was a pale, slender girl, with a sad face, and was dressed in rather shabby black. She had no special friend at Oaklawn, and the other girls did not know much about her. If they had thought about it at all, they would probably have decided that they did not like her; but for the most part they simply overlooked her.

This was not altogether their fault. Ruth was poor and apparently friendless, but it was not her poverty that was against her. Lou Scott, who was "as poor as a church mouse," to quote her own frank admission, was the most popular girl in the seminary, the boon companion of the richest girls, and in demand with everybody. But Lou was jolly and frank and offhanded, while Ruth was painfully shy and reserved, and that was the secret of the whole matter.

There was "no fun in her," the girls said, and so it came about that she was left out of their social life, and was almost as solitary at Oaklawn as if she had been the only girl there. She was there for the special purpose of studying music, and expected to earn her own living by teaching it when she left. She believed that the girls looked down on her on this account; this was unjust, of course, but Ruth had no idea how much her own coldness and reserve had worked against her.

Across the room Carol Golden was, as usual, the centre of an animated group; Golden Carol, as her particular friends sometimes called her, partly because of her beautiful voice, and partly because of her wonderful fleece of golden hair. Carol was one of the seminary pets, and seemed to Ruth Mannering to have everything that she had not.

Presently the mail was brought in, and there was a rush to the table, followed by exclamations of satisfaction or disappointment. In a few minutes the room was almost deserted. Only two girls remained: Carol Golden, who had dropped into a big chair to read her many letters; and Ruth Mannering, who had not received any and had gone silently back to her part of the window.

Presently Carol gave a little cry of delight. Her mother had written that she might invite any friend she wished home with her to spend the holidays. Carol had asked for this permission, and now that it had come was ready to dance for joy. As to whom she would ask, there could be only one answer to that. Of course it must be her particular friend, Maud Russell, who was the cleverest and prettiest girl at Oaklawn, at least so her admirers said. She was undoubtedly the richest, and was the acknowledged "leader." The girls affectionately called her "Princess," and Carol adored her with that romantic affection that is found only among school girls. She knew, too, that Maud would surely accept her invitation because she did not intend to go home. Her parents were travelling in Europe, and she expected to spend her holidays with some cousins, who were almost strangers to her.

Carol was so much pleased that she felt as if she must talk to somebody, so she turned to Ruth.

"Isn't it delightful to think that we'll all be going home in a fortnight?"

"Yes, very – for those that have homes to go to," said Ruth drearily.

Carol felt a quick pang of pity and self-reproach. "Haven't you?" she asked.

Ruth shook her head. In spite of herself, the kindness of Carol's tone brought the tears to her eyes.

"My mother died a year ago," she said in a trembling voice, "and since then I have had no real home. We were quite alone in the world, Mother and I, and now I have nobody."

"Oh, I'm so sorry for you," cried Carol impulsively. She leaned forward and took Ruth's hand in a gentle way. "And do you mean to say that you'll have to stay here all through the holidays? Why, it will be horrid."

"Oh, I shall not mind it much," said Ruth quickly, "with study and practice most of the time. Only now, when everyone is talking about it, it makes me wish that I had some place to go."

Carol dropped Ruth's hand suddenly in the shock of a sudden idea that darted into her mind.

A stray girl passing through the hall called out, "Ruth, Miss Siviter wishes to see you about something in Room C."

Ruth got up quickly. She was glad to get away, for it seemed to her that in another minute she would break down altogether.

Carol Golden hardly noticed her departure. She gathered up her letters and went abstractedly to her room, unheeding a gay call for "Golden Carol" from a group of girls in the corridor. Maud Russell was not in and Carol was glad. She wanted to be alone and fight down that sudden idea.

"It is ridiculous to think of it," she said aloud, with a petulance very unusual in Golden Carol, whose disposition was as sunny as her looks. "Why, I simply cannot. I have always been longing to ask Maud to visit me, and now that the chance has come I am not going to throw it away. I am very sorry for Ruth, of course. It must be dreadful to be all alone like that. But it isn't my fault. And she is so fearfully quiet and dowdy – what would they all think of her at home? Frank and Jack would make such fun of her. I shall ask Maud just as soon as she comes in."

Maud did come in presently, but Carol did not give her the invitation. Instead, she was almost snappish to her idol, and the Princess soon went out again in something of a huff.

"Oh, dear," cried Carol, "now I've offended her. What has got into me? What a disagreeable thing a conscience is, although I'm sure I don't know why mine should be prodding me so! I don't want to invite Ruth Mannering home with me for the holidays, but I feel exactly as if I should not have a minute's peace of mind all the time if I didn't. Mother would think it all right, of course. She would not mind if Ruth dressed in calico and never said anything but yes and no. But how the boys would laugh! I simply won't do it, conscience or no conscience."

In view of this decision it was rather strange that the next morning, Carol Golden went down to Ruth Mannering's lonely little room on Corridor Two and said, "Ruth, will you go home with me for the holidays? Mother wrote me to invite anyone I wished to. Don't say you can't come, dear, because you must."

Carol never, as long as she lived, forgot Ruth's face at that moment.

"It was absolutely transfigured," she said afterwards. "I never saw anyone look so happy in my life."

A FORTNIGHT LATER unwonted silence reigned at Oaklawn. The girls were scattered far and wide, and Ruth Mannering and Carol Golden were at the latter's home.

Carol was a very much surprised girl. Under the influence of kindness and pleasure Ruth seemed transformed into a different person. Her shyness and reserve melted away in the sunny atmosphere of the Golden home. Mrs. Golden took her into her motherly heart at once; and as for Frank and Jack, whose verdict Carol had so dreaded, they voted Ruth "splendid." She certainly got along very well with them; and if she did not make the social sensation that pretty Maud Russell might have made, the Goldens all liked her and Carol was content.

"Just four days more," sighed Carol one afternoon, "and then we must go back to Oaklawn. Can you realize it, Ruth?"

Ruth looked up from her book with a smile. Even in appearance she had changed. There was a faint pink in her cheeks and a merry light in her eyes.

"I shall not be sorry to go back to work," she said. "I feel just like it because I have had so pleasant a time here that it has heartened me up for next term. I think it will be very different from last. I begin to see that I kept to myself too much and brooded over fancied slights."

"And then you are to room with me since Maud is not coming back," said Carol. "What fun we shall have. Did you ever toast marshmallows over the gas? Why, I declare, there is Mr. Swift coming up the walk. Look, Ruth! He is the richest man in Westleigh."

Ruth peeped out of the window over Carol's shoulder.

"He reminds me of somebody," she said absently, "but I can't think who it is. Of course, I have never seen him before. What a good face he has!"

"He is as good as he looks," said Carol, enthusiastically. "Next to Father, Mr. Swift is the nicest man in the world. I have always been quite a pet of his. His wife is dead, and so is his only daughter. She was a lovely girl and died only two years ago. It nearly broke Mr. Swift's heart. And he has lived alone ever since in that great big house up at the head of Warner Street, the one you admired so, Ruth, the last time we were uptown. There's the bell for the second time, Mary can't have heard it. I'll go myself."

As Carol showed the caller into the room, Ruth rose to leave and thus came face to face with him. Mr. Swift started perceptibly.

"Mr. Swift, this is my school friend, Miss Mannering," said Carol.

Mr. Swift seemed strangely agitated as he took Ruth's timidly offered hand.

"My dear young lady," he said hurriedly, "I am going to ask you what may seem a very strange question. What was your mother's name?"

"Agnes Hastings," answered Ruth in surprise. And then Carol really thought that Mr. Swift had gone crazy, for he drew Ruth into his arms and kissed her.

"I knew it," he said. "I was sure you were Agnes' daughter, for you are the living image of what she was when I last saw her. Child, you don't know me, but I am your Uncle Robert. Your mother was my half-sister."

"Oh, Mr. Swift!" cried Carol, and then she ran for her mother.

Ruth turned pale and dropped into a chair, and Mr. Swift sat down beside her.

"To think that I have found you at last, child. How puzzled you look. Did your mother never speak of me? How is she? Where is she?"

"Mother died last year," said Ruth.

"Poor Agnes! And I never knew! Don't cry, little girl. I

want you to tell me all about it. She was much younger than I was, and when our mother died my stepfather went away and took her with him. I remained with my father's people and eventually lost all trace of my sister. I was a poor boy then, but things have looked up with me and I have often tried to find her."

By this time Carol had returned with her father and mother, and there was a scene – laughing, crying, explaining – and I don't really know which of the two girls was the more excited, Carol or Ruth. As for Mr. Swift, he was overjoyed to find his niece and wanted to carry her off with him then and there, but Mrs. Golden insisted on her finishing her visit. When the question of returning to Oaklawn came up, Mr. Swift would not hear of it at first, but finally yielded to Carol's entreaties and Ruth's own desire.

"I shall graduate next year, Uncle, and then I can come back to you for good."

That evening when Ruth was alone in her room, trying to collect her thoughts and realize that the home and love that she had so craved were really to be hers at last, Golden Carol was with her mother in the room below, talking it all over.

"Just think, Mother, if I had not asked Ruth to come here, this would not have happened. And I didn't want to, I wanted to ask Maud so much, and I was dreadfully disappointed when I couldn't – for I really couldn't. I could not help remembering the look in Ruth's eyes when she said that she had no home to go to, and so I asked her instead of Maud. How dreadful it would have been if I hadn't."

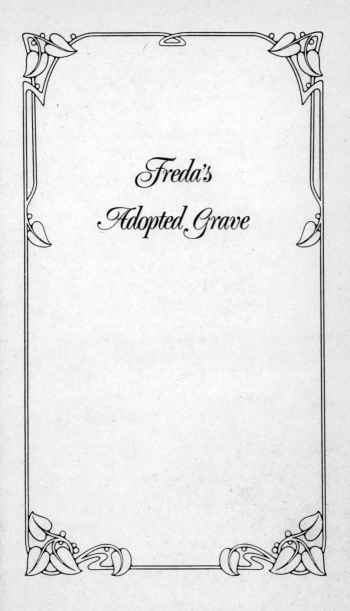

Freda's
Adopted Grave

ORTH POINT, where Freda lived, was the bleakest settlement in the world. Even its inhabitants, who loved it, had to admit that. The northeast winds swept whistling up the bay and blew rawly over the long hill that sloped down to it, blighting everything that was in their way. Only the sturdy firs and spruces could hold their own against it. So there were no orchards or groves or flower gardens in North Point.

Just over the hill, in a sheltered southwest valley, was the North Point church with the graveyard behind it, and this graveyard was the most beautiful spot in North Point or near it. The North Point folk loved flowers. They could not have them about their homes, so they had them in their graveyard. It was a matter of pride with each family to keep the separate plot neatly trimmed and weeded and adorned with beautiful blossoms.

It was one of the unwritten laws of the little community that on some selected day in May everybody would repair to the graveyard to plant, trim and clip. It was not an unpleasant duty, even to those whose sorrow was fresh. It seemed as if they were still doing something for the friends who had gone when they made their earthly resting places beautiful.

As for the children, they looked forward to "Graveyard Day" as a very delightful anniversary, and it divided its spring honours with the amount of the herring catch.

"Tomorrow is Graveyard Day," said Minnie Hutchinson at school recess, when all the little girls were sitting on the fence. "Ain't I glad! I've got the loveliest big white rosebush to plant by Grandma Hutchinson's grave. Uncle Robert sent it out from town."

"My mother has ten tuberoses to set out," said Nan Gray proudly.

"We're going to plant a row of lilies right around our plot," said Katie Morris.

Every little girl had some boast to make, that is, every little girl but Freda. Freda sat in a corner all by herself and felt miserably outside of everything. She had no part or lot in Graveyard Day.

"Are you going to plant anything, Freda?" asked Nan, with a wink at the others.

Freda shook her head mutely.

"Freda can't plant anything," said Winnie Bell cruelly, although she did not mean to be cruel. "She hasn't got a grave."

Just then Freda felt as if her gravelessness were a positive disgrace and crime, as if not to have an interest in a single grave in North Point cemetery branded you as an outcast forever and ever. It very nearly did in North Point. The other little girls pitied Freda, but at the same time they rather looked down upon her for it with the complacency of those who had been born into a good heritage of family graves and had an undisputed right to celebrate Graveyard Day.

Freda felt that her cup of wretchedness was full. She sat miserably on the fence while the other girls ran off to play, and she walked home alone at night. It seemed to her that she could *not* bear it any longer.

Freda was ten years old. Four years ago Mrs. Wilson had taken her from the orphan asylum in town. Mrs. Wilson lived just this side of the hill from the graveyard, and everybody in North Point called her a "crank." They pitied any child she took, they said. It would be worked to death and treated like a slave. At first they tried to pump Freda concerning Mrs. Wilson's treatment of her, but Freda was not to be pumped. She was a quiet little mite, with big, wistful dark eyes that had a disconcerting fashion of looking the gossips out of countenance. But if

Freda had been disposed to complain, the North Point people would have found out that they had been only too correct in their predictions.

"Mrs. Wilson," Freda said timidly that night, "why haven't we got a grave?"

Mrs. Wilson averred that such a question gave her the "creeps."

"You ought to be very thankful that we haven't," she said severely. "That Graveyard Day is a heathenish custom, anyhow. They make a regular picnic of it, and it makes me sick to hear those school girls chattering about what they mean to plant, each one trying to outblow the other. If I *had* a grave there, I wouldn't make a flower garden of it!"

Freda did not go to the graveyard the next day, although it was a holiday. But in the evening, when everybody had gone home, she crept over the hill and through the beech grove to see what had been done. The plots were all very neat and prettily set out with plants and bulbs. Some perennials were already in bud. The grave of Katie Morris' great-uncle, who had been dead for forty years, was covered with blossoming purple pansies. Every grave, no matter how small or old, had its share of promise – every grave except one. Freda came across it with a feeling of surprise. It was away down in the lower corner where there were no plots. It was shut off from the others by a growth of young poplars and was sunken and overgrown with blueberry shrubs. There was no headstone, and it looked dismally neglected. Freda felt a sympathy for it. She had no grave, and this grave had nobody to tend it or care for it.

When she went home she asked Mrs. Wilson whose it was.

"Humph!" said Mrs. Wilson. "If you have so much spare time lying round loose, you'd better put it into your sewing instead of prowling about graveyards. Do you expect me to work my fingers to the bone making clothes for you? I wish I'd left you in the asylum. That grave is Jordan Slade's, I suppose. He died twenty years ago, and a worthless, drunken scamp he was. He served a term in the penitentiary for breaking into Andrew Messervey's store, and after it he had the face to come back to North Point. But respectable people would have nothing to do with him, and he went to the dogs altogether – had to be buried on charity when he died. He hasn't any relations here. There was a sister, a little girl of ten, who used to live with the Cogswells over at East Point. After Jord died, some rich folks saw her and was so struck with her good looks that they took her away with them. I don't know what become of her, and I don't care. Go and bring the cows up."

When Freda went to bed that night her mind was made up. She would adopt Jordan Slade's grave.

Thereafter, Freda spent her few precious spare-time moments in the graveyard. She clipped the blueberry shrubs and long, tangled grasses from the grave with a pair of rusty old shears that blistered her little brown hands badly. She brought ferns from the woods to plant about it. She begged a root of heliotrope from Nan Gray, a clump of day lilies from Katie Morris, a rosebush slip from Nellie Bell, some pansy seed from old Mrs. Bennett, and a geranium shoot from Minnie Hutchinson's big sister. She planted, weeded and watered faithfully, and her efforts were rewarded. "Her" grave soon looked as nice as any in the graveyard.

Nobody but Freda knew about it. The poplar growth concealed the corner from sight, and everybody had quite forgotten poor, disreputable Jordan Slade's grave. At least, it seemed as if everybody had. But one evening, when Freda slipped down to the graveyard with a little can of water and rounded the corner of the poplars, she saw a lady standing by the grave – a strange lady dressed in black, with the loveliest face Freda had ever seen, and tears in her eyes.

The lady gave a little start when she saw Freda with her can of water.

"Can you tell me who has been looking after this grave?" she said.

"It – it was I," faltered Freda, wondering if the lady would be angry with her. "Pleas'm, it was I, but I didn't mean any harm. All the other little girls had a grave, and I hadn't any, so I just adopted this one."

"Did you know whose it was?" asked the lady gently.

"Yes'm – Jordan Slade's. Mrs. Wilson told me."

"Jordan Slade was my brother," said the lady. "He went sadly astray, but he was not all bad. He was weak and too easily influenced. But whatever his faults, he was good and kind – oh! so good and kind – to me when I was a child. I loved him with all my heart. It has always been my wish to come back and visit his grave, but I have never been able to come, my home has been so far away. I expected to find it neglected. I cannot tell you how pleased and touched I am to find it kept so beautifully. Thank you over and over again, my dear child!"

"Then you're not cross, ma'am?" said Freda eagerly. "And I may go on looking after it, may I? Oh, it just seems as if I couldn't bear not to!"

"You may look after it as long as you want to, my dear. I will help you, too. I am to be at East Point all summer. This will be our grave – yours and mine."

That summer was a wonderful one for Freda. She had found a firm friend in Mrs. Halliday. The latter was a wealthy woman. Her husband had died a short time previously and she had no children. When she went away in the fall, Freda went with her "to be her own little girl for always." Mrs. Wilson consented grudgingly to give Freda up, although she grumbled a great deal about ingratitude.

Before they went they paid a farewell visit to their grave. Mrs. Halliday had arranged with some of the North Point people to keep it well attended to, but Freda cried at leaving it.

"Don't feel badly about it, dear," comforted Mrs. Halliday. "We are coming back every summer to see it. It will always be our grave."

Freda slipped her hand into Mrs. Halliday's and smiled up at her.

"I'd never have found you, Aunty, if it hadn't been for this grave," she said happily. "I'm so glad I adopted it."

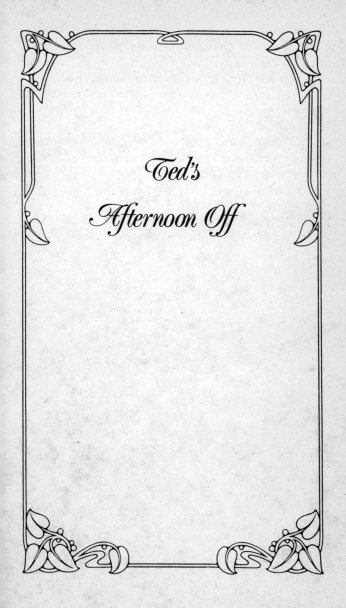

Ted's

Afternoon Off

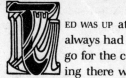ED WAS UP at five that morning, as usual. He always had to rise early to kindle the fire and go for the cows, but on this particular morning there was no "had to" about it. He had awakened at four o'clock and had sprung eagerly to the little garret window facing the east, to see what sort of a day was being born. Thrilling with excitement, he saw that it was going to be a glorious day. The sky was all rosy and golden and clear beyond the sharp-pointed, dark firs on Lee's Hill. Out to the north the sea was shimmering and sparkling gaily, with little foam crests here and there ruffled up by the cool morning breeze. Oh, it would be a splendid day!

And he, Ted Melvin, was to have a half holiday for the first time since he had come to live in Brookdale four years ago – a whole afternoon off to go to the Sunday School picnic at the beach beyond the big hotel. It almost seemed too good to be true!

The Jacksons, with whom he had lived ever since his mother had died, did not think holidays were necessities for boys. Hard work and cast-off clothes, and three grudgingly allowed months of school in the winter, made up Ted's life year in and year out – his outer life at least. He had an inner life of dreams, but nobody knew or suspected anything about that. To everybody in Brookdale he was simply Ted Melvin, a shy, odd-looking little fellow with big dreamy black eyes and a head of thick tangled curls which could never be made to look tidy and always annoyed Mrs. Jackson exceedingly.

It was as yet too early to light the fire or go for the cows. Ted crept softly to a corner in the garret and took from the wall an old brown fiddle. It had been his father's. He loved to play on it, and his few rare spare moments were always spent in the garret corner or the hayloft, with his precious fiddle. It was his one link with the old life he had lived in a little cottage far away, with a mother who had loved him and a merry young father who had made wonderful music on the old brown violin.

Ted pushed open his garret window and, seating himself on the sill, began to play, with his eyes fixed on the glowing eastern sky. He played very softly, since Mrs. Jackson had a pronounced dislike to being wakened by "fiddling at all unearthly hours."

The music he made was beautiful and would have astonished anybody who knew enough to know how wonderful it really was. But there was nobody to hear this little neglected urchin of all work, and he fiddled away happily, the music floating out of the garret window, over the treetops and the dew-wet clover fields, until it mingled with the winds and was lost in the silver skies of the morning.

Ted worked doubly hard all that forenoon, since there was a double share of work to do if, as Mrs. Jackson said, he was to be gadding to picnics in the afternoon. But he did it all cheerily and whistled for joy as he worked.

After dinner Mrs. Ross came in. Mrs. Ross lived down on the shore road and made a living for herself and her two children by washing and doing days' work out. She was not a very cheerful person and generally spoke as if on the point of bursting into tears. She looked more doleful than ever today, and lost no time in explaining why.

"I've just got word that my sister over at White Sands is sick with pendikis" – this was the nearest Mrs. Ross could get to appendicitis – "and has to go to the hospital. I've got to go right over and see her, Mrs. Jackson, and I've run in to ask if Ted can go and stay with Jimmy till I get back. There's no one else I can get, and Amelia is away. I'll be back this evening. I don't like leaving Jimmy alone."

"Ted's been promised that he could go to the picnic

this afternoon," said Mrs. Jackson shortly. "Mr. Jackson said he could go, so he'll have to please himself. If he's willing to stay with Jimmy instead, he can. *I* don't care."

"Oh, I've *got* to go to the picnic," cried Ted impulsively. "I'm awful sorry for Jimmy – but I *must* go to the picnic."

"I s'pose you feel so," said Mrs. Ross, sighing heavily. "I dunno's I blame you. Picnics is more cheerful than stay-ing with a poor little lame boy, I don't doubt. Well, I s'pose I can put Jimmy's supper on the table clost to him, and shut the cat in with him, and mebbe he'll worry through. He was counting on having you to fiddle for him, though. Jimmy's crazy about music, and he don't never hear much of it. Speaking of fiddling, there's a great fiddler stopping at the hotel now. His name is Blair Mil-ford, and he makes his living fiddling at concerts. I knew him well when he was a child – I was nurse in his father's family. He was a taking little chap, and I was real fond of him. Well, I must be getting. Jimmy'll feel bad at staying alone, but I'll tell him he'll just have to put up with it."

Mrs. Ross sighed herself away, and Ted flew up to his garret corner with a choking in his throat. He couldn't go to stay with Jimmy – he couldn't give up the picnic! Why, he had never been at a picnic; and they were going to drive to the hotel beach in wagons, and have swings, and games, and ice cream, and a boat sail to Curtain Island! He had been looking forward to it, waking and dreaming, for a fortnight. He *must* go. But poor little Jimmy! It *was* too bad for him to be left all alone.

"I wouldn't like it myself," said Ted miserably, trying to swallow a lump that persisted in coming up in his throat. "It must be dreadful to have to lie on the sofa all the time and never be able to run, climb trees or play, or do a single thing. And Jimmy doesn't like reading much. He'll be dreadful lonesome. I'll be thinking of him all the time at the picnic – I know I will. I suppose I *could* go and stay with him, if I just made up my mind to it."

Making up his mind to it was a slow and difficult process. But when Ted was finally dressed in his shabby, "skimpy" Sunday best, he tucked his precious fiddle under his arm and slipped downstairs. "Please, I think I'll go and stay with Jimmy," he said to Mrs. Jackson timidly, as he always spoke to her.

"Well, if you're to waste the afternoon, I s'pose it's better to waste it that way than in going to a picnic and eating yourself sick," was Mrs. Jackson's ungracious response.

Ted reached Mrs. Ross's little house just as that good lady was locking the door on Jimmy and the cat. "Well, I'm real glad," she said, when Ted told her he had come to stay. "I'd have worried most awful if I'd had to leave Jimmy all alone. He's crying in there this minute. Come now, Jimmy, dry up. Here's Ted come to stop with you after all, and he's brought his fiddle, too."

Jimmy's tears were soon dried, and he welcomed Ted joyfully. "I've been thinking awful long to hear you fiddling," said Jimmy, with a sigh of content. "Seems like the ache ain't never half so bad when I'm listening to music – and when it's your music, I forget there's any ache at all."

Ted took his violin and began to play. After all, it was almost as good as a picnic to have a whole afternoon for his music. The stuffy little room, with its dingy plaster and shabby furniture, was filled with wonderful harmonies. Once he began, Ted could play for hours at a stretch and never be conscious of fatigue. Jimmy lay and listened in rapturous content while Ted's violin sang and laughed and dreamed and rippled.

There was another listener besides Jimmy. Outside, on the red sandstone doorstep, a man was sitting – a tall, well-dressed man with a pale, beautiful face and long,

supple white hands. Motionless, he sat there and listened to the music until at last it stopped. Then he rose
and knocked at the door. Ted, violin in hand, opened it.

An expression of amazement flashed into the stranger's face, but he only said, "Is Mrs. Ross at home?"

"No, sir," said Ted shyly. "She went over to White Sands
and she won't be back till night. But Jimmy is here –
Jimmy is her little boy. Will you come in?"

"I'm sorry Mrs. Ross is away," said the stranger, enter-
ing. "She was an old nurse of mine. I must confess I've
been sitting on the step out there for some time, listening
to your music. Who taught you to play, my boy?"

"Nobody," said Ted simply. "I've always been able to
play."

"He makes it up himself out of his own head, sir," said
Jimmy eagerly.

"No, I don't make it – it makes itself – it just *comes*,"
said Ted, a dreamy gaze coming into his big black eyes.

The caller looked at him closely. "I know a little about
music myself," he said. "My name is Blair Milford and I
am a professional violinist. Your playing is wonderful.
What is your name?"

"Ted Melvin."

"Well, Ted, I think that you have a great talent, and it
ought to be cultivated. You should have competent in-
struction. Come, you must tell me all about yourself."

Ted told what little he thought there was to tell. Blair
Milford listened and nodded, guessing much that Ted
didn't tell and, indeed, didn't know himself. Then he
made Ted play for him again. "Amazing!" he said softly,
under his breath.

Finally he took the violin and played himself. Ted and
Jimmy listened breathlessly. "Oh, if I could only play like
that!" said Ted wistfully.

Blair Milford smiled. "You will play much better some

day if you get the proper training," he said. "You have a wonderful talent, my boy, and you should have it culti-vated. It will never in the world do to waste such genius. Yes, that is the right word," he went on musingly, as if talking to himself, " 'genius.' Nature is always taking us by surprise. This child has what I have never had and would make any sacrifice for. And yet in him it may come to naught for lack of opportunity. But it must not, Ted. You must have a musical training."

"I can't take lessons, if that is what you mean, sir," said Ted wonderingly. "Mr. Jackson wouldn't pay for them."

"I think we needn't worry about the question of pay-ment if you can find time to practise," said Blair Milford. "I am to be at the beach for two months yet. For once I'll take a music pupil. But will you have time to practise?"

"Yes, sir, I'll make time," said Ted, as soon as he could speak at all for the wonder of it. "I'll get up at four in the morning and have an hour's practising before the time for the cows. But I'm afraid it'll be too much trouble for you, sir, I'm afraid –"

Blair Milford laughed and put his slim white hand on Ted's curly head. "It isn't much trouble to train an artist. It is a privilege. Ah, Ted, you have what I once hoped I had, what I know now I never can have. You don't under-stand me. You will some day."

"Ain't he an awful nice man?" said Jimmy, when Blair Milford had gone. "But what did he mean by all that talk?"

"I don't know exactly," said Ted dreamily. "That is, I seem to *feel* what he meant but I can't quite put it into words. But, oh, Jimmy, I'm so happy. I'm to have les-sons – I have always longed to have them."

"I guess you're glad you didn't go to the picnic?" said Jimmy.

"Yes, but I was glad before, Jimmy, honest I was."

Blair Milford kept his promise. He interviewed Mr. and Mrs. Jackson and, by means best known to himself, induced them to consent that Ted should take music lessons every Saturday afternoon. He was a pupil to delight a teacher's heart and, after every lesson, Blair Milford looked at him with kindly eyes and murmured, "Amazing," under his breath. Finally he went again to the Jacksons, and the next day he said to Ted, "Ted, would you like to come away with me – live with me – be my boy and have your gift for music thoroughly cultivated?"

"What do you mean, sir?" said Ted tremblingly.

"I mean that I want you – that I must have you, Ted. I've talked to Mr. Jackson, and he has consented to let you come. You shall be educated, you shall have the best masters in your art that the world affords, you shall have the career I once dreamed of. Will you come, Ted?"

Ted drew a long breath. "Yes, sir," he said. "But it isn't so much because of the music – it's because I love you, Mr. Milford, and I'm so glad I'm to be always with you."

The Girl
Who Drove the Cows

"I WONDER WHO that pleasant-looking girl who drives cows down the beech lane every morning and evening is," said Pauline Palmer, at the tea table of the country farmhouse where she and her aunt were spending the summer. Mrs. Wallace had wanted to go to some fashionable watering place, but her husband had bluntly told her he couldn't afford it. Stay in the city when all her set were out she would not, and the aforesaid farmhouse had been the compromise.

"I shouldn't suppose it could make any difference to you who she is," said Mrs. Wallace impatiently. "I do wish, Pauline, that you were more careful in your choice of associates. You hobnob with everyone, even that old man who comes around buying eggs. It is very bad form."

Pauline hid a rather undutiful smile behind her napkin. Aunt Olivia's snobbish opinions always amused her.

"You've no idea what an interesting old man he is," she said. "He can talk more entertainingly than any other man I know. What is the use of being so exclusive, Aunt Olivia? You miss so much fun. You wouldn't be so horribly bored as you are if you fraternized a little with the 'natives,' as you call them."

"No, thank you," said Mrs. Wallace disdainfully.

"Well, I am going to try to get acquainted with that girl," said Pauline resolutely. "She looks nice and jolly."

"I don't know where you get your low tastes from," groaned Mrs. Wallace. "I'm sure it wasn't from your poor mother. What do you suppose the Morgan Knowles would think if they saw you taking up with some tomboy girl on a farm?"

"I don't see why it should make a great deal of difference what they would think, since they don't seem to be aware of my existence, or even of yours, Aunty," said Pauline, with twinkling eyes. She knew it was her aunt's dearest desire to get in with the Morgan Knowles' "set" – a desire that seemed as far from being realized as ever. Mrs. Wallace could never understand why the Morgan Knowles shut her from their charmed circle. They certainly associated with people much poorer and of more doubtful worldly station than hers – the Markhams, for instance, who lived on an unfashionable street and wore quite shabby clothes. Just before she had left Colchester, Mrs. Wallace had seen Mrs. Knowles and Mrs. Markham together in the former's automobile. James Wallace and Morgan Knowles were associated in business dealings; but in spite of Mrs. Wallace's schemings and aspirations and heart burnings, the association remained a purely business one and never advanced an inch in the direction of friendship.

As for Pauline, she was hopelessly devoid of social ambitions and she did not in the least mind the Morgan Knowles' remote attitude.

"Besides," continued Pauline, "she isn't a tomboy at all. She looks like a very womanly, well-bred sort of girl. Why should you think her a tomboy because she drives cows? Cows are placid, useful animals – witness this delicious cream which I am pouring over my blueberries. And they have to be driven. It's an honest occupation."

"I daresay she is someone's servant," said Mrs. Wallace contemptuously. "But I suppose even that wouldn't matter to you, Pauline?"

"Not a mite," said Pauline cheerfully. "One of the very nicest girls I ever knew was a maid Mother had the last year of her dear life. I loved that girl, Aunt Olivia, and I correspond with her. She writes letters that are ten times more clever and entertaining than those stupid epistles Clarisse Gray sends me – and Clarisse Gray is a rich man's daughter and is being educated in Paris."

"You are incorrigible, Pauline," said Mrs. Wallace hopelessly.

"Mrs. Boyd," said Pauline to their landlady, who now made her appearance, "who is that girl who drives the cows along the beech lane mornings and evenings?"

"Ada Cameron, I guess," was Mrs. Boyd's response. "She lives with the Embrees down on the old Embree place just below here. They're pasturing their cows on the upper farm this summer. Mrs. Embree is her father's half-sister."

"Is she as nice as she looks?"

"Yes, Ada's a real nice sensible girl," said Mrs. Boyd. "There is no nonsense about her."

"That doesn't sound very encouraging," murmured Pauline, as Mrs. Boyd went out. "I like people with a little nonsense about them. But I hope better things of Ada, Mrs. Boyd to the contrary notwithstanding. She has a pair of grey eyes that can't possibly always look sensible. I think they must mellow occasionally into fun and jollity and wholesome nonsense. Well, I'm off to the shore. I want to get that photograph of the Cove this evening, if possible. I've set my heart on taking first prize at the Amateur Photographers' Exhibition this fall, and if I can only get that Cove with all its beautiful lights and shadows, it will be the gem of my collection."

Pauline, on her return from the shore, reached the beech lane just as the Embree cows were swinging down it. Behind them came a tall, brown-haired, brown-faced girl in a neat print dress. Her hat was hung over her arm, and the low evening sunlight shone redly over her smooth glossy head. She carried herself with a pretty dignity, but when her eyes met Pauline's, she looked as if she would smile on the slightest provocation.

Pauline promptly gave her the provocation.

"Good evening, Miss Cameron," she called blithely. "Won't you please stop a few moments and look me over? I want to see if you think me a likely person for a summer chum."

Ada Cameron did more than smile. She laughed outright and went over to the fence where Pauline was sitting on a stump. She looked down into the merry black eyes of the town girl she had been half envying for a week and said humorously: "Yes, I think you very likely, indeed. But it takes two to make a friendship – like a bargain. If I'm one, you'll have to be the other."

"I'm the other. Shake," said Pauline, holding out her hand.

That was the beginning of a friendship that made poor Mrs. Wallace groan outwardly as well as inwardly. Pauline and Ada found that they liked each other even more than they had expected to. They walked, rowed, berried and picnicked together. Ada did not go to Mrs. Boyd's a great deal, for some instinct told her that Mrs. Wallace did not look favourably on her, but Pauline spent half her time at the little, brown, orchard-embowered house at the end of the beech lane where the Embrees lived. She had never met any girl she thought so nice as Ada.

"She is nice every way," she told the unconvinced Aunt Olivia. "She's clever and well read. She is sensible and frank. She has a sense of humour and a great deal of insight into character – witness her liking for your niece! She can talk interestingly and she can also be silent when silence is becoming. And she has the finest profile I ever saw. Aunt Olivia, may I ask her to visit me next winter?"

"No, indeed," said Mrs. Wallace, with crushing emphasis. "You surely don't expect to continue this absurd intimacy past the summer, Pauline?"

"I expect to be Ada's friend all my life," said Pauline

78

laughingly, but with a little ring of purpose in her voice. "Oh, Aunty, dear, can't you see that Ada is just the same girl in cotton print that she would be in silk attire? She is really far more distinguished looking than any girl in the Knowles' set."

"Pauline!" said Aunt Olivia, looking as shocked as if Pauline had committed blasphemy.

Pauline laughed again, but she sighed as she went to her room. Aunt Olivia has the kindest heart in the world, she thought. What a pity she isn't able to see things as they really are! My friendship with Ada can't be perfect if I can't invite her to my home. And she is such a dear girl – the first real friend after my own heart that I've ever had.

The summer waned, and August burned itself out.

"I suppose you will be going back to town next week? I shall miss you dreadfully," said Ada.

The two girls were in the Embree garden, where Pauline was preparing to take a photograph of Ada standing among the asters, with a great sheaf of them in her arms. Pauline wished she could have said: But you must come and visit me in the winter. Since she could not, she had to content herself with saying: "You won't miss me any more than I shall miss you. But we'll correspond, and I hope Aunt Olivia will come to Marwood again next summer."

"I don't think I shall be here then," said Ada with a sigh. "You see, it is time I was doing something for myself, Pauline. Aunt Jane and Uncle Robert have always been very kind to me, but they have a large family and are not very well off. So I think I'll try for a situation in one of the Remington stores this fall."

"It's such a pity you couldn't have gone to the Academy and studied for a teacher's licence," said Pauline, who knew what Ada's ambitions were.

"I should have liked that better, of course," said Ada quietly. "But it is not possible, so I must do my best at the next best thing. Don't let's talk of it. It might make me feel blueish and I want to look especially pleasant if I'm going to have my photo taken."

"You couldn't look anything else," laughed Pauline. "Don't smile too broadly – I want you to be looking over the asters with a bit of a dream on your face and in your eyes. If the picture turns out as beautiful as I fondly expect, I mean to put it in my exhibition collection under the title 'A September Dream.' There, that's the very expression. When you look like that, you remind me of somebody I have seen, but I can't remember who it is. All ready now – don't move – there, dearie, it is all over."

When Pauline went back to Colchester, she was busy for a month preparing her photographs for the exhibition, while Aunt Olivia renewed her spinning of all the little social webs in which she fondly hoped to entangle the Morgan Knowles and other desirable flies.

When the exhibition was opened, Pauline Palmer's collection won first prize, and the prettiest picture in it was one called "A September Dream" – a tall girl with a wistful face, standing in an old-fashioned garden with her arms full of asters.

The very day after the exhibition was opened the Morgan Knowles' automobile stopped at the Wallace door. Mrs. Wallace was out, but it was Pauline whom stately Mrs. Morgan Knowles asked for. Pauline was at that moment buried in her darkroom developing photographs, and she ran down just as she was – a fact which would have mortified Mrs. Wallace exceedingly if she had ever known it. But Mrs. Morgan Knowles did not seem to mind at all. She liked Pauline's simplicity of manner. It was more than she had expected from the aunt's rather vulgar affectations.

"I have called to ask you who the original of the photograph 'A September Dream' in your exhibit was, Miss Palmer," she said graciously. "The resemblance to a very dear childhood friend of mine is so startling that I am sure it cannot be accidental."

"That is a photograph of Ada Cameron, a friend whom I met this summer up in Marwood," said Pauline.

"Ada Cameron! She must be Ada Frame's daughter, then," exclaimed Mrs. Knowles in excitement. Then, seeing Pauline's puzzled face, she explained: "Years ago, when I was a child, I always spent my summers on the farm of my uncle, John Frame. My cousin, Ada Frame, was the dearest friend I ever had, but after we grew up we saw nothing of each other, for I went with my parents to Europe for several years, and Ada married a neighbour's son, Alec Cameron, and went out west. Her father, who was my only living relative other than my parents, died, and I never heard anything more of Ada until about eight years ago, when somebody told me she was dead and had left no family. That part of the report cannot have been true if this girl is her daughter."

"I believe she is," said Pauline quickly. "Ada was born out west and lived there until she was eight years old, when her parents died and she was sent east to her father's half-sister. And Ada looks like you – she always reminded me of somebody I had seen, but I never could decide who it was before. Oh, I hope it is true, for Ada is such a sweet girl, Mrs. Knowles."

"She couldn't be anything else if she is Ada Frame's daughter," said Mrs. Knowles. "My husband will investigate the matter at once, and if this girl is Ada's child we shall hope to find a daughter in her, as we have none of our own."

"What will Aunt Olivia say!" said Pauline with wickedly dancing eyes when Mrs. Knowles had gone.

Aunt Olivia was too much overcome to say anything. That good lady felt rather foolish when it was proved that the girl she had so despised was Mrs. Morgan Knowles' cousin and was going to be adopted by her. But to hear Aunt Olivia talk now, you would suppose that she and not Pauline had discovered Ada.

The latter sought Pauline out as soon as she came to Colchester, and the summer friendship proved a life-long one and was, for the Wallaces, the open sesame to the enchanted ground of the Knowles' "set."

"So everybody concerned is happy," said Pauline. "Ada is going to college and so am I, and Aunt Olivia is on the same committee as Mrs. Knowles for the big church bazaar. What about my 'low tastes' now, Aunt Olivia?"

"Well, who would ever have supposed that a girl who drove cows to pasture was connected with the Morgan Knowles?" said poor Aunt Olivia piteously.

Why Not Ask Miss Price?

RANCES ALLEN came in from the post office and laid an open letter on the table beside her mother, who was making mincemeat. Alma Allen looked up from the cake she was frosting to ask, "What is the matter? You look as if your letter contained unwelcome news, Fan."

"So it does. It is from Aunt Clara, to say she cannot come. She has received a telegram that her sister-in-law is very ill and she must go to her at once."

Mrs. Allen looked regretful, and Alma cast her spoon away with a tragic air.

"That is too bad. I feel as if our celebration were spoiled. But I suppose it can't be helped."

"No," agreed Frances, sitting down and beginning to peel apples. "So there is no use in lamenting, or I would certainly sit down and cry, I feel so disappointed."

"Is Uncle Frank coming?"

"Yes, Aunt Clara says he will come down from Stellarton if Mrs. King does not get worse. So that will leave just one vacant place. We must invite someone to fill it up. Who shall it be?"

Both girls looked rather puzzled. Mrs. Allen smiled a quiet little smile all to herself and went on chopping suet. She had handed the Thanksgiving dinner over to Frances and Alma this year. They were to attend to all the preparations and invite all the guests. But although they had made or planned several innovations in the dinner itself, they had made no change in the usual list of guests.

"It must just be the time-honoured family affair," Frances had declared. "If we begin inviting other folks, there is no knowing when to draw the line. We can't have more than fourteen, and some of our friends would be sure to feel slighted."

So the same old list it was. But now Aunt Clara – dear, jolly Aunt Clara, whom everybody in the connection loved and admired – could not come, and her place must be filled.

"We can't invite the new minister, because we would have to have his sister, too," said Frances. "And there is no reason for asking any one of our girl chums more than another."

"Mother, you will have to help us out," said Alma. "Can't you suggest a substitute guest?"

Mrs. Allen looked down at the two bright, girlish faces turned up to her and said slowly, "I think I can, but I am not sure my choice will please you. Why not ask Miss Price?"

Miss Price! They had never thought of her! She was the pale, timid-looking little teacher in the primary department of the Hazelwood school.

"Miss Price?" repeated Frances slowly. "Why, Mother, we hardly know her. She is dreadfully dull and quiet, I think."

"And so shy," said Alma. "Why, at the Wards' party the other night she looked startled to death if anyone spoke to her. I believe she would be frightened to come here for Thanksgiving."

"She is a very lonely little creature," said Mrs. Allen gently, "and doesn't seem to have anyone belonging to her. I think she would be very glad to get an invitation to spend Thanksgiving elsewhere than in that cheerless little boarding-house where she lives."

"Of course, if you would like to have her, Mother, we will ask her," said Frances.

"No, girls," said Mrs. Allen seriously. "You must not ask Miss Price on my account, if you do not feel prepared to make her welcome for her own sake. I had hoped that your own kind hearts might have prompted you to extend a little Thanksgiving cheer in a truly Thanksgiving spirit to a lonely, hard-working girl whose life I do not think is a happy one. But there, I shall not preach. This is your dinner, and you must please yourselves as to your guests."

Frances and Alma had both flushed, and they now remained silent for a few minutes. Then Frances sprang up and threw her arms around her mother.

"You're right, Mother dear, as you always are, and we are very selfish girls. We will ask Miss Price and try to give her a nice time. I'll go down this very evening and see her."

IN THE GREY TWILIGHT of the chilly autumn evening Bertha Price walked home to her boarding-house, her pale little face paler, and her grey eyes sadder than ever, in the fading light. Only two days until Thanksgiving – but there would be no real Thanksgiving for her. Why, she asked herself rebelliously, when there seemed so much love in the world, was she denied her share?

Her landlady met her in the hall.

"Miss Allen is in the parlour, Miss Price. She wants to see you."

Bertha went into the parlour somewhat reluctantly. She had met Frances Allen only once or twice and she was secretly almost afraid of the handsome, vivacious girl who was so different from herself.

"I am sorry you have had to wait, Miss Allen," she said shyly. "I went to see a pupil of mine who is ill and I was kept later than I expected."

"My errand won't take very long," said Frances brightly. "Mother wants you to spend Thanksgiving Day with us, Miss Price, if you have no other engagement. We will have a few other guests, but nobody outside our own family except Mr. Seeley, who is the law partner and intimate friend of my brother Ernest in town. You'll come, won't you?"

"Oh, thank you, yes," said Bertha, in pleased surprise. "I shall be very glad to go. Why, it is so nice to think of it. I expected my Thanksgiving Day to be lonely and sad – not a bit Thanksgivingy."

"We shall expect you then," said Frances, with a cordial little hand-squeeze. "Come early in the morning, and we will have a real friendly, pleasant day."

That night Frances said to her mother and sister, "You never saw such a transfigured face as Miss Price's when I asked her up. She looked positively pretty – such a lovely pink came out on her cheeks and her eyes shone like stars. She reminded me so much of somebody I've seen, but I can't think who it is. I'm so glad we've asked her here for Thanksgiving!"

THANKSGIVING CAME, as bright and beautiful as a day could be, and the Allens' guests came with it. Bertha Price was among them, paler and shyer than ever. Ernest Allen and his friend, Maxwell Seeley, came out from town on the morning train.

After all the necessary introductions had been made, Frances flew to the kitchen.

"I've found out who it is Miss Price reminds me of," she said, as she bustled about the range. "It's Max Seeley. You needn't laugh, Al. It's a fact. I noticed it the minute I introduced them. He's plump and prosperous and she's pinched and pale, but there's a resemblance nevertheless. Look for yourself and see if it isn't so."

Back in the big, cheery parlour the Thanksgiving guests were amusing themselves in various ways. Max Seeley had given an odd little start when he was introduced to Miss Price, and as soon as possible he followed her to the corner where she had taken refuge. Ernest

Allen was out in the kitchen talking to his sisters, the "uncles and cousins and aunts" were all chattering to each other, and Mr. Seeley and Miss Price were quite unnoticed.

"You will excuse me, won't you, Miss Price, if I ask you something about yourself?" he said eagerly. "The truth is, you look so strikingly like someone I used to know that I feel sure you must be related to her. I do not think I have any relatives of your name. Have you any of mine?"

Bertha flushed, hesitated for an instant, then said frankly, "No, I do not think so. But I may as well tell you that Price is not my real name and I do not know what it is, although I think it begins with S. I believe that my parents died when I was about three years old, and I was then taken to an orphan asylum. The next year I was taken from there and adopted by Mrs. Price. She was very kind to me and treated me as her own daughter. I had a happy home with her, although we were poor. Mrs. Price wished me to bear her name, and I did so. She never told me my true surname, perhaps she did not know it. She died when I was sixteen, and since then I have been quite alone in the world. That is all I know about myself."

Max Seeley was plainly excited.

"Why do you think your real name begins with S?" he asked.

"I have a watch which belonged to my mother, with the monogram 'B.S.' on the case. It was left with the matron of the asylum and she gave it to Mrs. Price for me. Here it is."

Max Seeley almost snatched the old-fashioned little silver watch from her hand and opened the case. An exclamation escaped him as he pointed to some scratches on the inner side. They looked like the initials M.A.S.

"Let me tell my story now," he said. "My name is Maxwell Seeley. My father died when I was seven years old, and my mother a year later. My little sister, Bertha, then three years old, and I were left quite alone and very poor. We had no relatives. I was adopted by a well-to-do old bachelor, who had known my father. My sister was taken to an orphan asylum in a city some distance away. I was very much attached to her and grieved bitterly over our parting. My adopted father was very kind to me and gave me a good education. I did not forget my sister, and as soon as I could I went to the asylum. I found that she had been taken away long before, and I could not even discover who had adopted her, for the original building, with all its records, had been destroyed by fire two years previous to my visit. I never could find any clue to her whereabouts, and long since gave up all hope of finding her. But I have found her at last. You are Bertha Seeley, my little sister!"

"Oh – can it be possible!"

"More than possible – it is certain. You are the image of my mother, as I remember her, and as an old daguerreotype I have pictures her. And this is her watch – see, I scratched my own initials on the case one day. There is no doubt in the world. Oh, Bertha, are you half as glad as I am?"

"Glad!"

Bertha's eyes were shining like stars. She tried to smile, but burst into tears instead and her head went down on her brother's shoulder. By this time everybody in the room was staring at the extraordinary tableau, and Ernest, coming through the hall, gave a whistle of astonishment that brought the two in the corner back to a sense of their surroundings.

"I haven't suddenly gone crazy, Ernest, old fellow," smiled Max. "Ladies and gentlemen all, this little schoolma'am was introduced to you as Miss Price, but that was a mistake. Let me introduce her again as Miss Bertha Seeley, my long-lost and newly-found sister."

Well, they had an amazing time then, of course. They laughed and questioned and explained until the dinner was in imminent danger of getting stone-cold on the dining-room table. Luckily, Alma and Frances remembered it just in the nick of time, and they all got out, somehow, and into their places. It was a splendid dinner, but I believe that Maxwell and Bertha Seeley didn't know what they were eating, any more than if it had been sawdust. However, the rest of the guests made up for that, and did full justice to the girls' cookery.

In the afternoon they all went to church, and at least two hearts were truly and devoutly thankful that day.

When the dusk came, Ernest and Maxwell had to catch the last train for town, and the other guests went home, with the exception of Bertha, who was to stay all night. Just as soon as her resignation could be effected, she was to join her brother.

"Meanwhile, I'll see about getting a house to put you in," said Max. "No more boarding out for me, Ernest. You may consider me as a family man henceforth."

Frances and Alma talked it all over before they went to sleep that night.

"Just think," said Frances, "if we hadn't asked her here today she might never have found her brother! It's all Mother's doing, bless her! Things do happen like a storybook sometimes, don't they, Al? And didn't I tell you they looked alike?"

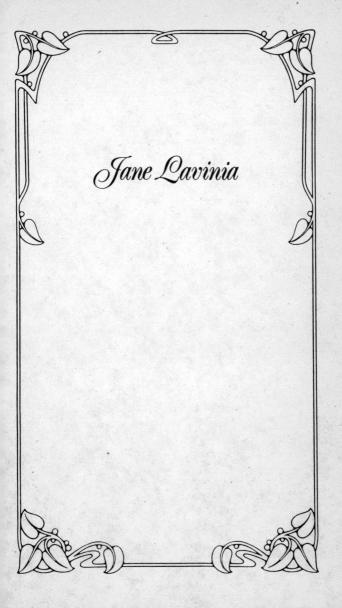

Jane Lavinia

ANE LAVINIA put her precious portfolio down on the table in her room, carefully, as if its contents were fine gold, and proceeded to unpin and take off her second-best hat. When she had gone over to the Whittaker place that afternoon, she had wanted to wear her best hat, but Aunt Rebecca had vetoed that uncompromisingly.

"Next thing you'll be wanting to wear your best muslin to go for the cows," said Aunt Rebecca sarcastically. "You go right back upstairs and take off that chiffon hat. If I was fool enough to be coaxed into buying it for you, I ain't going to have you spoil it by traipsing hither and yon with it in the dust and sun. Your last summer's sailor is plenty good enough to go to the Whittakers' in, Jane Lavinia."

"But Mr. Stephens and his wife are from New York," pleaded Jane Lavinia, "and she's so stylish."

"Well, it's likely they're used to seeing chiffon hats," Aunt Rebecca responded, more sarcastically than ever. "It isn't probable that yours would make much of a sensation. Mr. Stephens didn't send for you to show him your chiffon hat, did he? If he did, I don't see what you're lugging that big portfolio along with you for. Go and put on your sailor hat, Jane Lavinia."

Jane Lavinia obeyed. She always obeyed Aunt Rebecca. But she took off the chiffon hat and pinned on the sailor with bitterness of heart. She had always hated that sailor. Anything ugly hurt Jane Lavinia with an intensity that Aunt Rebecca could never understand; and the sailor hat was ugly, with its stiff little black bows and impossible blue roses. It jarred on Jane Lavinia's artistic instincts. Besides, it was very unbecoming.

I look horrid in it, Jane Lavinia had thought sorrowfully; and then she had gone out and down the velvet-green springtime valley and over the sunny birch hill beyond with a lagging step and a rebellious heart.

But Jane Lavinia came home walking as if on the clear air of the crystal afternoon, her small, delicate face aglow and every fibre of her body and spirit thrilling with excitement and delight. She forgot to fling the sailor hat into its box with her usual energy of dislike. Just then Jane Lavinia had a soul above hats. She looked at herself in the glass and nodded with friendliness.

"You'll do something yet," she said. "Mr. Stephens said you would. Oh, I like you, Jane Lavinia, you dear thing! Sometimes I haven't liked you because you're nothing to look at, and I didn't suppose you could really do anything worthwhile. But I do like you now after what Mr. Stephens said about your drawings."

Jane Lavinia smiled radiantly into the little cracked glass. Just then she was pretty, with the glow on her cheeks and the sparkle in her eyes. Her uncertainly tinted hair and an all-too-certain little tilt of her nose no longer troubled her. Such things did not matter; nobody would mind them in a successful artist. And Mr. Stephens had said that she had talent enough to win success.

Jane Lavinia sat down by her window, which looked west into a grove of firs. They grew thickly, close up to the house, and she could touch their wide, fan-like branches with her hand. Jane Lavinia loved those fir trees, with their whispers and sighs and beckonings, and she also loved her little shadowy, low-ceilinged room, despite its plainness, because it was gorgeous for her with visions and peopled with rainbow fancies.

The stained walls were covered with Jane Lavinia's pictures – most of them pen-and-ink sketches, with a few flights into water colour. Aunt Rebecca sniffed at them and deplored the driving of tacks into the plaster. Aunt Rebecca thought Jane Lavinia's artistic labours a flat waste of time, which would have been much better put into rugs and crochet tidies and afghans. All the other girls in Chestercote made rugs and tidies and afghans. Why must Jane Lavinia keep messing with ink and crayons and water colours?

Jane Lavinia only knew that she *must* – she could not help it. There was something in her that demanded expression thus.

When Mr. Stephens, who was a well-known artist and magazine illustrator, came to Chestercote because his wife's father, Nathan Whittaker, was ill, Jane Lavinia's heart had bounded with a shy hope. She indulged in some harmless manoeuvring which, with the aid of good-natured Mrs. Whittaker, was crowned with success. One day, when Mr. Whittaker was getting better, Mr. Stephens had asked her to show him some of her work. Jane Lavinia, wearing the despised sailor hat, had gone over to the Whittaker place with some of her best sketches. She came home again feeling as if all the world and herself were transfigured.

She looked out from the window of her little room with great dreamy brown eyes, seeing through the fir boughs the golden western sky beyond, serving as a canvas whereon her fancy painted glittering visions of her future. She would go to New York – and study – and work, oh, so hard – and go abroad – and work harder – and win success – and be great and admired and famous – if only Aunt Rebecca – ah! if only Aunt Rebecca! Jane Lavinia sighed. There was spring in the world and spring in Jane Lavinia's heart; but a chill came with the thought of Aunt Rebecca, who considered tidies and afghans nicer than her pictures.

"But I'm going, anyway," said Jane Lavinia decidedly. "If Aunt Rebecca won't give me the money, I'll find some other way. I'm not afraid of any amount of work. After what Mr. Stephens said, I believe I could work twenty hours out of the twenty-four. I'd be content to live on a crust and sleep in a garret – yes, and wear sailor hats with stiff bows and blue roses the year round."

Jane Lavinia sighed in luxurious renunciation. Oh, it was good to be alive – to be a girl of seventeen, with wonderful ambitions and all the world before her! The years of the future sparkled and gleamed alluringly. Jane Lavinia, with her head on the window sill, looked out into the sunset splendour and dreamed.

Athwart her dreams, rending in twain their frail, rose-tinted fabric, came Aunt Rebecca's voice from the kitchen below, "Jane Lavinia! Jane Lavinia! Ain't you going for the cows tonight?"

Jane Lavinia started up guiltily; she had forgotten all about the cows. She slipped off her muslin dress and hurried into her print; but with all her haste it took time, and Aunt Rebecca was grimmer than ever when Jane Lavinia ran downstairs.

"It'll be dark before we get the cows milked. I s'pose you've been day-dreaming again up there. I do wish, Jane Lavinia, that you had more sense."

Jane Lavinia made no response. At any other time she would have gone out with a lump in her throat; but now, after what Mr. Stephens had said, Aunt Rebecca's words had no power to hurt her.

"After milking I'll ask her about it," she said to herself, as she went blithely down the sloping yard, across the little mossy bridge over the brook, and up the lane on the hill beyond, where the ferns grew thickly and the grass was beset with tiny blue-eyes like purple stars. The air was moist and sweet. At the top of the lane a wild plum tree hung out its branches of feathery bloom against the crimson sky. Jane Lavinia lingered, in spite of Aunt Rebecca's hurry, to look at it. It satisfied her artistic instinct and made her glad to be alive in the world where wild plums blossomed against springtime skies. The pleasure of it went with her through the pasture and back to the milking yard, and stayed with her while she helped Aunt Rebecca milk the cows.

When the milk was strained into the creamers down at the spring, and the pails washed and set in a shining row on their bench, Jane Lavinia tried to summon up her courage to speak to Aunt Rebecca. They were out on the back verandah; the spring twilight was purpling down over the woods and fields; down in the swamp the frogs were singing a silvery, haunting chorus; a little baby moon was floating in the clear sky above the white-blossoming orchard on the slope.

Jane Lavinia tried to speak and couldn't. For a wonder, Aunt Rebecca spared her the trouble.

"Well, what did Mr. Stephens think of your pictures?" she asked shortly.

"Oh!" Everything that Jane Lavinia wanted to say came rushing at once and together to her tongue's end. "Oh, Aunt Rebecca, he was delighted with them! And he said I had remarkable talent, and he wants me to go to New York and study in an art school there. He says Mrs. Stephens finds it hard to get good help, and if I'd be willing to work for her in the mornings, I could live with them and have my afternoons off. So it won't cost much. And he said he would help me – and, oh, Aunt Rebecca, can't I go?"

Jane Lavinia's breath gave out with a gasp of suspense.

Aunt Rebecca was silent for so long a space that Jane Lavinia had time to pass through the phases of hope and fear and despair and resignation before she said, more grimly than ever, "If your mind is set on going, go you will, I suppose. It doesn't seem to me that I have anything to say in the matter, Jane Lavinia."

"But, oh, Aunt Rebecca," said Jane Lavinia tremulously. "I can't go unless you'll help me. I'll have to pay for my lessons at the art school, you know."

"So that's it, is it? And do you expect me to give you the money to pay for them, Jane Lavinia?"

"Not give – exactly," stammered Jane Lavinia. "I'll pay it back some time, Aunt Rebecca. Oh, indeed, I will – when I'm able to earn money by my pictures!"

"The security is hardly satisfactory," said Aunt Rebecca immovably. "You know well enough I haven't much money, Jane Lavinia. I thought when I was coaxed into giving you two quarters' lessons with Miss Claxton that it was as much as you could expect me to do for you. I didn't suppose the next thing would be that you'd be for betaking yourself to New York and expecting me to pay your bills there."

Aunt Rebecca turned and went into the house. Jane Lavinia, feeling sore and bruised in spirit, fled to her own room and cried herself to sleep.

Her eyes were swollen the next morning, but she was not sulky. Jane Lavinia never sulked. She did her morning's work faithfully, although there was no spring in her step. That afternoon, when she was out in the orchard trying to patch up her tattered dreams, Aunt Rebecca came down the blossomy avenue, a tall, gaunt figure, with an uncompromising face.

"You'd better go down to the store and get ten yards of white cotton, Jane Lavinia," she said. "If you're going to New York, you'll have to get a supply of underclothing made."

Jane Lavinia opened her eyes.

"Oh, Aunt Rebecca, am I going?"

"You can go if you want to. I'll give you all the money I can spare. It ain't much, but perhaps it'll be enough for a start."

"Oh, Aunt Rebecca, thank you!" exclaimed Jane Lavinia, crimson with conflicting feelings. "But perhaps I oughtn't to take it – perhaps I oughtn't to leave you alone –"

If Aunt Rebecca had shown any regret at the thought of Jane Lavinia's departure, Jane Lavinia would have foregone New York on the spot. But Aunt Rebecca only said coldly, "I guess you needn't worry over that. I can get along well enough."

And with that it was settled. Jane Lavinia lived in a whirl of delight for the next week. She felt few regrets at leaving Chestercote. Aunt Rebecca would not miss her; Jane Lavinia thought that Aunt Rebecca regarded her as a nuisance – a foolish girl who wasted her time making pictures instead of doing something useful. Jane Lavinia had never thought that Aunt Rebecca had any affection for her. She had been a very little girl when her parents had died, and Aunt Rebecca had taken her to bring up. Accordingly she had been "brought up," and she was grateful to Aunt Rebecca, but there was no closer bond between them. Jane Lavinia would have given love for love unstintedly, but she never supposed that Aunt Rebecca loved her.

On the morning of departure Jane Lavinia was up and ready early. Her trunk had been taken over to Mr. Whittaker's the night before, and she was to walk over in the morning and go with Mr. and Mrs. Stephens to the station. She put on her chiffon hat to travel in, and Aunt Rebecca did not say a word of protest. Jane Lavinia cried when she said good-by, but Aunt Rebecca did not cry. She shook hands and said stiffly, "Write when you get to New York. You needn't let Mrs. Stephens work you to death either."

Jane Lavinia went slowly over the bridge and up the lane. If only Aunt Rebecca had been a little sorry! But the morning was perfect and the air clear as crystal, and she was going to New York, and fame and fortune were to be hers for the working. Jane Lavinia's spirits rose and bubbled over in a little trill of song. Then she stopped in dismay. She had forgotten her watch – her mother's little gold watch; she had left it on her dressing table.

Jane Lavinia hurried down the lane and back to the house. In the open kitchen doorway she paused, standing on a mosaic of gold and shadow where the sunshine fell through the morning-glory vines. Nobody was in the kitchen, but Aunt Rebecca was in the little bedroom that opened off it, crying bitterly and talking aloud between her sobs, "Oh, she's gone and left me all alone – my girl has gone! Oh, what shall I do? And she didn't care – she was glad to go – glad to get away. Well, it ain't any wonder. I've always been too cranky with her. But I loved her so much all the time, and I was so proud of her! I liked her picture-making real well, even if I did complain of her wasting her time. Oh, I don't know how I'm ever going to keep on living now she's gone!"

Jane Lavinia listened with a face from which all the sparkle and excitement had gone. Yet amid all the wreck and ruin of her tumbling castles in air, a glad little thrill made itself felt. Aunt Rebecca was sorry – Aunt Rebecca did love her after all!

Jane Lavinia turned and walked noiselessly away. As she went swiftly up the wild plum lane, some tears brimmed up in her eyes, but there was a smile on her lips and a song in her heart. After all, it was nicer to be loved than to be rich and admired and famous.

When she reached Mr. Whittaker's, everybody was out in the yard ready to start.

"Hurry up, Jane Lavinia," said Mr. Whittaker. "Blest if we hadn't begun to think you weren't coming at all. Lively now."

"I am not going," said Jane Lavinia calmly.

"Not going?" they all exclaimed.

"No. I'm very sorry, and very grateful to you, Mr. Stephens, but I can't leave Aunt Rebecca. She'd miss me too much."

"Well, you little goose!" said Mrs. Whittaker.

Mrs. Stephens said nothing, but frowned coldly. Perhaps her thoughts were less of the loss to the world of art than of the difficulty of hunting up another housemaid. Mr. Stephens looked honestly regretful.

"I'm sorry, very sorry, Miss Slade," he said. "You have exceptional talent, and I think you ought to cultivate it."

"I am going to cultivate Aunt Rebecca," said Jane Lavinia.

Nobody knew just what she meant, but they all understood the firmness of her tone. Her trunk was taken down out of the express wagon, and Mr. and Mrs. Stephens drove away. Then Jane Lavinia went home. She found Aunt Rebecca washing the breakfast dishes, with the big tears rolling down her face.

"Goodness me!" she cried, when Jane Lavinia walked in. "What's the matter? You ain't gone and been too late!"

"No, I've just changed my mind, Aunt Rebecca. They've gone without me. I am not going to New York – I don't want to go. I'd rather stay at home with you."

For a moment Aunt Rebecca stared at her. Then she stepped forward and flung her arms about the girl.

"Oh, Jane Lavinia," she said with a sob, "I'm so glad! I couldn't see how I was going to get along without you, but I thought you didn't care. You can wear that chiffon hat everywhere you want to, and I'll get you a pink organdy dress for Sundays."

SHE EYED CHESTER SOURLY.

The Running Away
of Chester

"I HAD A LITTLE BOY ONCE WHO USED TO
SLEEP HERE," SHE SAID.

HESTER did the chores with unusual vim that night. His lips were set and there was an air of resolution as plainly visible on his small, freckled face as if it had been stamped there. Mrs. Elwell saw him flying around, and her grim features took on a still grimmer expression.

"Ches is mighty lively tonight," she muttered. "I s'pose he's in a gog to be off on some foolishness with Henry Wilson. Well, he won't, and he needn't think it."

Lige Barton, the hired man, also thought this was Chester's purpose, but he took a more lenient view of it than did Mrs. Elwell.

"The little chap is going through things with a rush this evening," he reflected. "Guess he's laying out for a bit of fun with the Wilson boy."

But Chester was not planning anything connected with Henry Wilson, who lived on the other side of the pond and was the only chum he possessed. After the chores were done, he lingered a little while around the barns, getting his courage keyed up to the necessary pitch.

Chester Stephens was an orphan without kith or kin in the world, unless his father's stepsister, Mrs. Harriet Elwell, could be called so. His parents had died in his babyhood, and Mrs. Elwell had taken him to bring up. She was a harsh woman, with a violent temper, and she had scolded and worried the boy all his short life. Upton people said it was a shame, but nobody felt called upon to interfere. Mrs. Elwell was not a person one would care to make an enemy of.

She eyed Chester sourly when he went in, expecting some request to be allowed to go with Henry, and prepared to refuse it sharply.

"Aunt Harriet," said Chester suddenly, "can I go to school this year? It begins tomorrow."

"No," said Mrs. Elwell, when she had recovered from her surprise at this unexpected question. "You've had schoolin' in plenty – more'n I ever had, and all you're goin' to get!"

"But, Aunt Harriet," persisted Chester, his face flushed with earnestness, "I'm nearly thirteen, and I can barely read and write a little. The other boys are ever so far ahead of me. I don't know anything."

"You know enough to be disrespectful!" exclaimed Mrs. Elwell. "I suppose you want to go to school to idle away your time, as you do at home – lazy good-for-nothing that you are!" Chester thought of the drudgery that had been his portion all his life. He resented being called lazy when he was willing enough to work, but he made one more appeal.

"If you'll let me go to school this year, I'll work twice as hard out of school to make up for it – indeed, I will. Do let me go, Aunt Harriet. I haven't been to school a day for over a year."

"Let's hear no more of this nonsense," said Mrs. Elwell, taking a bottle from the shelf above her with the air of one who closes a discussion. "Here, run down to the Bridge and get me this bottle full of vinegar at Jacob's store. Be smart, too, d'ye hear! I ain't going to have you idling around the Bridge neither. If you ain't back in twenty minutes, it won't be well for you."

Chester did his errand at the Bridge with a heart full of bitter disappointment and anger.

"I won't stand it any longer!" he muttered. "I'll run away – I don't care where, so long as it's away from her. I wish I could get out West on the harvest excursions."

On his return home, as he crossed the yard in the dusk, he stumbled over a stick of wood and fell. The bottle of vinegar slipped from his hand and was broken on the doorstep. Mrs. Elwell saw the accident from the window. She rushed out and jerked the unlucky lad to his feet.

"Take that, you sulky little cub!" she exclaimed, cuffing his ears soundly. "I'll teach you to break and spill things you're sent for! You did it on purpose. Get off to bed with you this instant."

Chester crept off to his garret chamber with a very sullen face. He was too used to being sent to bed without any supper to care much for that, although he was hungry. But his whole being was in a tumult of rebellion over the injustice that was meted out to him.

"I won't stand it!" he muttered over and over again. "I'll run away. I won't stay here."

To talk of running away was one thing. To do it without a cent in your pocket or a place to run to was another. But Chester had a great deal of determination in his make-up when it was fairly roused, and his hard upbringing had made him older and shrewder than his years. He lay awake late that night, thinking out ways and means, but could arrive at no satisfactory conclusion.

The next day Mrs. Elwell said, "Ches, Abner Stearns wants you to go up there for a fortnight while Tom Bixby is away, and drive the milk wagon of mornings and do the chores for Mrs. Stearns. You might as well put in the time 'fore harvest that way as any other. So hustle off – and mind you behave yourself."

Chester heard the news gladly. He had not yet devised any feasible plan for running away, and he always liked to work at the Stearns' place. To be sure, Mrs. Elwell received all the money he earned, but Mrs. Stearns was kind to him, and though he had to work hard and constantly, he was well fed and well treated by all.

The following fortnight was a comparatively happy one

for the lad. But he did not forget his purpose of shaking the dust of Upton from his feet as soon as possible, and he cudgelled his brains trying to find a way.

On the evening when he left the Stearns' homestead, Mr. Stearns paid him for his fortnight's work, much to the boy's surprise, for Mrs. Elwell had always insisted that all such money should be paid directly to her. Chester found himself the possessor of four dollars – an amount of riches that almost took away his breath. He had never in his whole life owned more than ten cents at a time. As he tramped along the road home, he kept his hand in his pocket, holding fast to the money, as if he feared it would otherwise dissolve into thin air.

His mind was firmly made up. He would run away once and for all. This money was rightly his; he had earned every cent of it. It would surely last him until he found employment elsewhere. At any rate, he would go; and even if he starved, he would never come back to Aunt Harriet's!

When he reached home, he found Mrs. Elwell in an unusual state of worry. Lige had given warning – and this on the verge of harvest!

"Did Stearns say anything about coming down tomorrow to pay me for your work?" she asked.

"No, ma'am. He didn't say a word about it," said Chester boldly.

"Well, I hope he will. Take yourself off to bed, Ches. I'm sick of seeing you standing there, on one foot or t'other, like a gander."

Chester had been shifting about uneasily. He realized that, if his project did not miscarry, he would not see his aunt again, and his heart softened to her. Harsh as she was, she was the only protector he had ever known, and the boy had a vague wish to carry away with him some kindly word or look from her. Such, however, was not forthcoming, and Chester obeyed her command and took himself off to the garret. Here he sat down and reflected on his plans.

He must go that very night. When Mr. Stearns failed to appear on the morrow, Mrs. Elwell was quite likely to march up and demand the amount of Chester's wages. It would all come out then, and he would lose his money – besides, no doubt, getting severely punished into the bargain.

His preparations did not take long. He had nothing to carry with him. The only decent suit of clothes he possessed was his well-worn Sunday one. This he put on, carefully stowing away in his pocket the precious four dollars.

He had to wait until he thought his aunt was asleep, and it was about eleven when he crept downstairs, his heart quaking within him, and got out by the porch window. When he found himself alone in the clear moonlight of the August night, a sense of elation filled his cramped little heart. He was free, and he would never come back here – never!

"Wisht I could have seen Henry to say good-by to him, though," he muttered with a wistful glance at the big house across the pond where the unconscious Henry was sleeping soundly with never a thought of moonlight flittings for anyone in his curly head.

Chester meant to walk to Roxbury Station ten miles away. Nobody knew him there, and he could catch the morning train. Late as it was, he kept to fields and wood-roads lest he might be seen and recognized. It was three o'clock when he reached Roxbury, and he knew the train did not pass through until six. With the serenity of a philosopher who is starting out to win his way in the world and means to make the best of things, Chester curled himself up in the hollow space of a big lumber pile behind the station, and so tired was he that he fell soundly asleep in a few minutes.

CHESTER WAS AWAKENED by the shriek of the express at the last crossing before the station. In a panic of haste he scrambled out of his lumber and dashed into the station house, where a sleepy, ill-natured agent stood behind the ticket window. He looked sharply enough at the freckled, square-jawed boy who asked for a second-class ticket to Belltown. Chester's heart quaked within him at the momentary thought that the ticket agent recognized him. He had an agonized vision of being collared without ceremony and haled straightway back to Aunt Harriet. When the ticket and his change were pushed out to him, he snatched them and fairly ran.

"Bolted as if the police were after him," reflected the agent, who did not sell many tickets and so had time to take a personal interest in the purchasers thereof. "I've seen that youngster before, though I can't recollect where. He's got a most fearful determined look."

Chester drew an audible sigh of relief when the train left the station. He was fairly off now and felt that he could defy even curious railway officials.

It was not his first train ride, for Mrs. Elwell had once taken him to Belltown to get an aching tooth extracted, but it was certainly his first under such exhilarating circumstances, and he meant to enjoy it. To be sure, he was very hungry, but that, he reflected, was only what he would probably be many times before he made his fortune, and it was just as well to get used to it. Meanwhile, it behooved him to keep his eyes open. On the road from Roxbury to Belltown there was not much to be seen that morning that Chester did not see.

The train reached Belltown about noon. He did not mean to stop long there – it was too near Upton. From the conductor on the train, he found that a boat left Belltown for Montrose at two in the afternoon. Montrose was a hundred miles from Upton, and Chester thought he would be safe there. To Montrose, accordingly, he decided to go, but the first thing was to get some dinner. He went into a grocery store and bought some crackers and a bit of cheese. He had somewhere picked up the idea that crackers and cheese were about as economical food as you could find for adventurous youths starting out on small capital.

He found his way to the only public square Belltown boasted, and munched his food hungrily on a bench under the trees. He would go to Montrose and there find something to do. Later on he would gradually work his way out West, where there was more room for an ambitious small boy to expand and grow. Chester dreamed some dazzling dreams as he sat there on the bench under the Belltown chestnuts. Passers-by, if they noticed him at all, saw merely a rather small, poorly clad boy, with a great many freckles, a square jaw and shrewd, level-gazing grey eyes. But this same lad was mapping out a very brilliant future for himself as people passed him heedlessly by. He would get out West, somehow or other, some time or other, and make a fortune. Then, perhaps, he would go back to Upton for a visit and shine in his splendour before all his old neighbours. It all seemed very easy and alluring, sitting there in the quiet little Belltown square. Chester, you see, possessed imagination. That, together with the crackers and cheese, so cheered him up that he felt ready for anything. He was aroused from a dream of passing Aunt Harriet by in lofty scorn and a glittering carriage, by the shrill whistle of the boat. Chester pocketed his remaining crackers and cheese and his visions also, and was once more his alert, wide-awake self. He had inquired the way to the wharf from the grocer, so he found no difficulty in reaching it. When the boat steamed down the muddy little river, Chester was on board of her.

He was glad to be out of Belltown, for he was anything but sure that he would not encounter some Upton people as long as he was in it. They often went to Belltown on business, but never to Montrose.

There were not many passengers on the boat, and Chester scrutinized them all so sharply in turn that he could have sworn to each and every one of them for years afterwards had it been necessary. The one he liked best was a middle-aged lady who sat just before him on the opposite side of the deck. She was plump and motherly looking, with a fresh, rosy face and beaming blue eyes.

"If I was looking for anyone to adopt me I'd pick her," said Chester to himself. The more he looked at her, the better he liked her. He labelled her in his mind as "the nice, rosy lady."

The nice, rosy lady noticed Chester staring at her after awhile. She smiled promptly at him – a smile that seemed fairly to irradiate her round face – and then began fumbling in an old-fashioned reticule she carried, and from which she presently extracted a chubby little paper bag.

"If you like candy, little boy," she said to Chester, "here is some of my sugar taffy for you."

Chester did not exactly like being called a little boy. But her voice and smile were irresistible and won his heart straightway. He took the candy with a shy, "Thank you, ma'am," and sat holding it in his hand.

"Eat it," commanded the rosy lady authoritatively. "That is what taffy is for, you know."

So Chester ate it. It was the most delicious thing he had ever tasted in his life, and filled a void which even the crackers and cheese had left vacant. The rosy lady watched every mouthful he ate as if she enjoyed it more than he did. When he had finished the taffy she smiled one of her sociable smiles again and said, "Well, what do you think of it?"

"It's the nicest taffy I ever ate," answered Chester enthusiastically, as if he were a connoisseur in all kinds of taffies. The rosy lady nodded, well pleased.

"That is just what everyone says about my sugar taffy. Nobody up our way can match it, though goodness knows they try hard enough. My great-grandmother invented the recipe herself, and it has been in our family ever since. I'm real glad you liked it."

She smiled at him again, as if his appreciation of her taffy was a bond of good fellowship between them. She did not know it but, nevertheless, she was filling the heart of a desperate small boy, who had run away from home, with hope and encouragement and self-reliance. If there were such kind folks as this in the world, why, he would get along all right. The rosy lady's smiles and taffy – the smiles much more than the taffy – went far to thaw out of him a certain hardness and resentfulness against people in general that Aunt Harriet's harsh treatment had instilled into him. Chester instantly made a resolve that when he grew stout and rosy and prosperous he would dispense smiles and taffy and good cheer generally to all forlorn small boys on boats and trains.

It was almost dark when they reached Montrose. Chester lost sight of the rosy lady when they left the boat, and it gave him a lonesome feeling; but he could not indulge in that for long at a time. Here he was at his destination – at dark, in a strange city a hundred miles from home.

"The first thing is to find somewhere to sleep," he said to himself, resolutely declining to feel frightened, although the temptation was very strong.

Montrose was not really a very big place. It was only a

bustling little town of some twenty thousand inhabitants, but to Chester's eyes it was a vast metropolis. He had never been in any place bigger than Belltown, and in Belltown you could see one end of it, at least, no matter where you were. Montrose seemed endless to Chester as he stood at the head of Water Street and gazed in bewilderment along one of its main business avenues – a big, glittering, whirling place where one small boy could so easily be swallowed up that he would never be heard of again.

Chester, after paying his fare to Montrose and buying his cheese and crackers, had just sixty cents left. This must last him until he found work, so that the luxury of lodgings was out of the question, even if he had known where to look for them. To be sure, there were benches in a public square right in front of him; but Chester was afraid that if he curled up on one of them for the night, a policeman might question him, and he did not believe he could give a very satisfactory account of himself. In his perplexity, he thought of his cosy lumber pile at Roxbury Station and remembered that when he had left the boat he had noticed a large vacant lot near the wharf which was filled with piles of lumber. Back to this he went and soon succeeded in finding a place to stow himself. His last waking thought was that he must be up and doing bright and early the next morning, and that it must surely be longer than twenty-four hours since he had crept downstairs and out of Aunt Harriet's porch window at Upton.

MONTROSE SEEMED less alarming by daylight, which was not so bewildering as the blinking electric lights. Chester was up betimes, ate the last of his cheese and crackers and started out at once to look for work. He determined to be thorough, and he went straight into every place of business he came to, from a blacksmith's forge to a department store, and boldly asked the first person he met if they wanted a boy there. There was, however, one class of places Chester shunned determinedly. He never went into a liquor saloon. The last winter he had been allowed to go to school in Upton, his teacher had been a pale, patient little woman who hated the liquor traffic with all her heart. She herself had suffered bitterly through it, and she instilled into her pupils a thorough aversion to it. Chester would have chosen death by starvation before he would have sought for employment in a liquor saloon. But there certainly did not seem room for him anywhere else. Nobody wanted a boy. The answer to his question was invariably "No." As the day wore on, Chester's hopes and courage went down to zero, but he still tramped doggedly about. He would be thorough, at least. Surely somewhere in this big place, where everyone seemed so busy, there must be something for him to do.

Once there seemed a chance of success. He had gone into a big provision store and asked the clerk behind the counter if they wanted a boy.

"Well, we do," said the clerk, looking him over critically, "but I hardly think you'll fill the bill. However, come in and see the boss."

He took Chester into a dark, grimy little inner office where a fat, stubby man was sitting before a desk with his feet upon it.

"Hey? What!" he said when the clerk explained. "Looking for the place? Why, sonny, you're not half big enough."

"Oh, I'm a great deal bigger than I look," cried Chester breathlessly. "That is, sir – I mean I'm ever so much stronger than I look. I'll work hard, sir, ever so hard – and I'll grow."

The fat, stubby man roared with laughter. What was

grim earnest to poor Chester was a joke to him.

"No doubt you will, my boy," he said genially, "but I'm afraid you'll hardly grow fast enough to suit us. Boys aren't like pigweed, you know. No, no, our boy must be a big, strapping fellow of eighteen or nineteen. He'll have a deal of heavy lifting to do."

Chester went out of the store with a queer choking in his throat. For one horrible moment he thought he was going to cry – he, Chester Stephens, who had run away from home to do splendid things! A nice ending that would be to his fine dreams! He thrust his hands into his pockets and strode along the street, biting his lips fiercely. He would not cry – no, he would not! And he *would* find work!

Chester did not cry, but neither, alas, did he find work. He parted with ten cents of his precious hoard for more crackers, and he spend the night again in the lumber yard.

Perhaps I'll have better luck tomorrow, he thought hopefully.

But it really seemed as if there were to be no luck for Chester except bad luck. Day after day passed and, although he tramped resolutely from street to street and visited every place that seemed to offer any chance, he could get no employment. In spite of his pluck, his heart began to fail him.

At the end of a week Chester woke up among his lumber to a realization that he was at the end of his resources. He had just five cents left out of the four dollars that were to have been the key to his fortune. He sat gloomily on the wall of his sleeping apartment and munched the one solitary cracker he had left. It must carry him through the day unless he got work. The five cents must be kept for some dire emergency.

He started uptown rather aimlessly. In his week's

wanderings he had come to know the city very well and no longer felt confused with its size and bustle. He envied every busy boy he saw. Back in Upton he had sometimes resented the fact that he was kept working continually and was seldom allowed an hour off. Now he was burdened with spare time. It certainly did not seem as if things were fairly divided, he thought. And then he thought no more just then, for one of the queer spells in his head came on. He had experienced them at intervals during the last three days. Something seemed to break loose in his head and spin wildly round and round, while houses and people and trees danced and wobbled all about him. Chester vaguely wondered if this could be what Aunt Harriet had been wont to call a "judgement." But then, he had done nothing very bad – nothing that would warrant a judgement, he thought. It was surely no harm to run away from a place where you were treated so bad and where they did not seem to want you. Chester felt bitter whenever he thought of Aunt Harriet.

Presently he found himself in the market square of Montrose. It was market day, and the place was thronged with people from the surrounding country settlements. Chester had hoped that he might pick up a few cents, holding a horse or cow for somebody or carrying a market basket, but no such chance offered itself. He climbed up on some bales of pressed hay in one corner and sat there moodily; there was dejection in the very dangle of his legs over the bales. Chester, you see, was discovering what many a boy before him has discovered – that it is a good deal easier to sit down and make a fortune in dreams than it is to go out into the world and make it.

Two men were talking to each other near him. At first Chester gave no heed to their conversation, but presently a sentence made him prick up his ears.

"Yes, there's a pretty fair crop out at Hopedale," one man was saying, "but whether it's going to be got in in good shape is another matter. It's terrible hard to get any help. Every spare man-jack far and wide has gone West on them everlasting harvest excursions. Salome Whitney at the Mount Hope Farm is in a predicament. She's got a hired man, but he can't harvest grain all by himself. She spent the whole of yesterday driving around, trying to get a couple of men or boys to help him, but I dunno if she got anyone or not."

The men moved out of earshot at this juncture, but Chester got down from the bales with a determined look. If workers were wanted in Hopedale, that was the place for him. He had done a man's work at harvest time in Upton the year before. Lige Barton had said so himself. Hope and courage returned with a rush.

He accosted the first man he met and asked if he could tell him the way to Hopedale.

"Reckon I can, sonny. I live in the next district. Want to go there? If you wait till evening, I can give you a lift part of the way. It's five miles out."

"Thank you, sir," said Chester firmly, "but I must go at once if you'll kindly direct me. It's important."

"Well, it's a straight road. That's Albemarle Street down there – follow it till it takes you out to the country, and then keep straight on till you come to a church painted yellow and white. Turn to your right, and over the hill is Hopedale. But you'd better wait for me. You don't look fit to walk five miles."

But Chester was off. Walk five miles! Pooh! He could walk twenty with hope to lure him on. Albemarle Street finally frayed off into a real country road. Chester was glad to find himself out in the country once more, with the great golden fields basking on either side and the wooded hills beyond, purple with haze. He had grown to hate the town with its cold, unheeding faces. It was good to breathe clear air again and feel the soft, springy soil of the ferny roadside under his tired little feet.

Long before the five miles were covered, Chester began to wonder if he would hold out to the end of them. He had to stop and rest frequently, when those queer dizzy spells came on. His feet seemed like lead. But he kept doggedly on. He would not give in now! The white and yellow church was the most welcome sight that had ever met his eyes.

Over the hill he met a man and inquired the way to Mount Hope Farm. Fortunately, it was nearby. At the gate Chester had to stop again to recover from his dizziness.

He liked the look of the place, with its great, comfortable barns and quaint, roomy old farmhouse, all set down in a trim quadrangle of beeches and orchards. There was an appearance of peace and prosperity about it.

If only Miss Salome Whitney will hire me! thought Chester wistfully, as he crept up the slope. I'm afraid she'll say I'm too small. Wisht I could stretch three inches all at once. Wisht I wasn't so dizzy. Wisht –

What Chester's third wish was will never be known, for just as he reached the kitchen door the worst dizzy spell of all came on. Trees, barns, well-sweep, all whirled around him with the speed of wind. He reeled and fell, a limp, helpless little body, on Miss Salome Whitney's broad, spotless sandstone doorstep.

IN THE MOUNT HOPE KITCHEN Miss Salome was at that moment deep in discussion with her "help" over the weighty question of how the damsons were to be preserved. Miss Salome wanted them boiled; Clemantiny Bosworth, the help, insisted that they ought to be baked. Clemantiny was always very positive. She had "bossed"

Miss Salome for years, and both knew that in the end the damsons would be baked, but the argument had to be carried out for dignity's sake.

"They're so sour when they're baked," protested Miss Salome.

"Well, you don't want damsons sweet, do you?" retorted Clemantiny scornfully. "That's the beauty of damsons – their tartness. And they keep ever so much better baked, Salome – you know they do. My grandmother *always* baked hers, and they would keep for three years."

Miss Salome knew that when Clemantiny dragged her grandmother into the question, it was time to surrender. Beyond that, dignity degenerated into stubbornness. It would be useless to say that she did not want to keep her damsons for three years, and that she was content to eat them up and trust to Providence for the next year's supply.

"Well, well, bake them then," she said placidly. "I don't suppose it makes much difference one way or another. Only, I insist – what was that noise, Clemantiny? It sounded like something falling against the porch door."

"It's that worthless dog of Martin's, I suppose," said Clemantiny, grasping a broom handle with a grimness that boded ill for the dog. "Mussing up my clean doorstep with his dirty paws again. I'll fix him!"

Clemantiny swept out through the porch and jerked open the door. There was a moment's silence. Then Miss Salome heard her say, "For the land's sake! Salome Whitney, come here."

What Miss Salome saw when she hurried out was a white-faced boy stretched on the doorstep at Clemantiny's feet.

"Is he dead?" she gasped.

"Dead? No," sniffed Clemantiny. "He's fainted, that's

what he is. Where on earth did he come from? He ain't a Hopedale boy."

"He must be carried right in," exclaimed Miss Salome in distress. "Why, he may die there. He must be very ill."

"Looks more to me as if he had fainted from sheer starvation," returned Clemantiny brusquely as she picked him up in her lean, muscular arms. "Why, he's skin and bone. He ain't hardly heavier than a baby. Well, this is a mysterious piece of work. Where'll I put him?"

"Lay him on the sofa," said Miss Salome as soon as she had recovered from the horror into which Clemantiny's starvation dictum had thrown her. A child starving to death on her doorstep! "What do you do for people in a faint, Clemantiny?"

"Wet their face – and hist up their feet – and loosen their collar," said Clemantiny in a succession of jerks, doing each thing as she mentioned it. "And hold ammonia to their nose. Run for the ammonia, Salome. Look, will you? Skin and bone!"

But Miss Salome had gone for the ammonia. There was a look on the boy's thin, pallid face that tugged painfully at her heart-strings.

When Chester came back to consciousness with the pungency of the ammonia reeking through his head, he found himself lying on very soft pillows in a very big white sunny kitchen, where everything was scoured to a brightness that dazzled you. Bending over him was a tall, gaunt woman with a thin, determined face and snapping black eyes, and, standing beside her with a steaming bowl in her hand, was the nice rosy lady who had given him the taffy on the boat!

When he opened his eyes, Miss Salome knew him.

"Why, it's the little boy I saw on the boat!" she exclaimed.

"Well, you've come to!" said Clemantiny, eyeing Chester severely. "And now perhaps you'll explain what you mean by fainting away on doorsteps and scaring people out of their senses."

Chester thought that this must be the mistress of Mount Hope Farm, and hastened to propitiate her.

"I'm sorry," he faltered feebly. "I didn't mean to – I –"

"You're not to do any talking until you've had something to eat," snapped Clemantiny inconsistently. "Here, open your mouth and take this broth. Pretty doings, I say!"

Clemantiny spoke as sharply as Aunt Harriet had ever done, but somehow or other Chester did not feel afraid of her and her black eyes. She sat down by his side and fed him from the bowl of hot broth with a deft gentleness oddly in contrast with her grim expression.

Chester thought he had never in all his life tasted anything so good as that broth. The boy was really almost starved. He drank every drop of it. Clemantiny gave a grunt of satisfaction as she handed the empty bowl and spoon to the silent, smiling Miss Salome.

"Now, who are you and what do you want?" she said.

Chester had been expecting this question, and while coming along the Hopedale road he had thought out an answer to it. He began now, speaking the words slowly and gaspingly, as if reciting a hastily learned lesson.

"My name is Chester Benson. I belong to Upton up the country. My folks are dead and I came to Montrose to look for work. I've been there a week and couldn't get anything to do. I heard a man say that you wanted men to help in the harvest, so I came out to see if you'd hire me."

In spite of his weakness, Chester's face turned very red before he got to the end of his speech. He was new to deception. To be sure, there was not, strictly speaking, an untrue word in it. As for his name, it was Chester Benson Stephens. But for all that, Chester could not have felt or looked more guilty if he had been telling an out-and-out falsehood at every breath.

"Humph!" said Clemantiny in a dissatisfied tone. "What on earth do you suppose a midget like you can do in the harvest field? And we don't want any more help, anyway. We've got enough."

Chester grew sick with disappointment. But at this moment Miss Salome spoke up.

"No, we haven't, Clemantiny. We want another hand, and I'll hire you, Chester – that's your name, isn't it? I'll give you good wages, too."

"Now, Salome!" protested Clemantiny.

But Miss Salome only said, "I've made up my mind, Clemantiny."

Clemantiny knew that when Miss Salome did make up her mind and announced it in that very quiet, very unmistakable tone, she was mistress of the situation and intended to remain so.

"Oh, very well," she retorted. "You'll please yourself, Salome, of course. *I* think it would be wiser to wait until you found out a little more about him."

"And have him starving on people's doorsteps in the meantime?" questioned Miss Salome severely.

"Well," returned Clemantiny with the air of one who washes her hands of a doubtful proposition, "don't blame me if you repent of it."

By this time Chester had grasped the wonderful fact that his troubles were ended – for a while, at least. He raised himself up on one arm and looked gratefully at Miss Salome.

"Thank you," he said. "I'll work hard. I'm used to doing a lot."

"There, there!" said Miss Salome, patting his shoulder

gently. "Lie down and rest. Dinner will be ready soon, and I guess you'll be ready for it."

To Clemantiny she added in a low, gentle tone, "There's a look on his face that reminded me of Johnny. It came out so strong when he sat up just now that it made me feel like crying. Don't you notice it, Clemantiny?"

"Can't say that I do," replied that energetic person, who was flying about the kitchen with a speed that made Chester's head dizzy trying to follow her with his eyes. "All I can see is freckles and bones – but if you're satisfied, I am. For law's sake, don't fluster me, Salome. There's a hundred and one things to be done out of hand. This frolic has clean dundered the whole forenoon's work."

After dinner Chester decided that it was time to make himself useful.

"Can't I go right to work now?" he asked.

"We don't begin harvest till tomorrow," said Miss Salome. "You'd better rest this afternoon."

"Oh, I'm all right now," insisted Chester. "I feel fine. Please give me something to do."

"You can go out and cut me some wood for my afternoon's baking," said Clemantiny. "And see you cut it short enough. Any other boy that's tried always gets it about two inches too long."

When he had gone out, she said scornfully to Miss Salome, "Well, what do you expect that size to accomplish in a harvest field, Salome Whitney?"

"Not very much, perhaps," said Miss Salome mildly. "But what could I do? You wouldn't have me turn the child adrift on the world again, would you, Clemantiny?"

Clemantiny did not choose to answer this appeal. She rattled her dishes noisily into the dishpan.

"Well, where are you going to put him to sleep?" she

demanded. "The hands you've got will fill the kitchen chamber. There's only the spare room left. You'll hardly put him there, I suppose? Your philanthropy will hardly lead you as far as *that*."

When Clemantiny employed big words and sarcasm at the same time, the effect was tremendous. But Miss Salome didn't wilt.

"What makes you so prejudiced against him?" she asked curiously.

"I'm *not* prejudiced against him. But that story about himself didn't ring true. I worked in Upton years ago, and there weren't any Bensons there then. There's more behind that he hasn't told. I'd find out what it was before I took him into my house, that's all. But I'm not prejudiced."

"Well, well," said Miss Salome soothingly, "we must do the best we can for him. It's a sort of duty. And as for a room for him – why, I'll put him in Johnny's."

Clemantiny opened her mouth and shut it again. She understood that it would be a waste of breath to say anything more. If Miss Salome had made up her mind to put this freckled, determined-looking waif, dropped on her doorstep from heaven knew where, into Johnny's room, that was an end of the matter.

"But I'll not be surprised at anything after this," she muttered as she carried her dishes into the pantry. "First a skinny little urchin goes and faints on her doorstep. Then she hires him and puts him in Johnny's room. Johnny's room! Salome Whitney, what *do* you mean?"

Perhaps Miss Salome hardly knew what she meant. But somehow her heart went out warmly to this boy. In spite of Clemantiny's sniffs, she held to the opinion that he looked like Johnny. Johnny was a little nephew of hers. She had taken him to bring up when his parents died, and she had loved him very dearly. He had died four years ago, and since that time the little front room over the front porch had never been occupied. It was just as Johnny had left it. Beyond keeping it scrupulously clean, Miss Salome never allowed it to be disturbed. And now a somewhat ragged lad from nowhere was to be put into it! No wonder Clemantiny shook her head when Miss Salome went up to air it.

EVEN CLEMANTINY had to admit that Chester was willing to work. He split wood until she called him to stop. Then he carried in the wood-box full, and piled it so neatly that even the grim handmaiden was pleased. After that, she sent him to the garden to pick the early beans. In the evening he milked three cows and did all the chores, falling into the ways of the place with a deft adaptability that went far to soften Clemantiny's heart.

"He's been taught to work somewheres," she admitted grudgingly, "and he's real polite and respectful. But he looks too cute by half. And his name isn't Benson any more than mine. When I called him 'Chester Benson' out there in the cow-yard, he stared at me fer half a minute 'sif I'd called him Nebuchadnezzar."

When bedtime came, Miss Salome took Chester up to a room whose whiteness and daintiness quite took away the breath of a lad who had been used to sleeping in garrets or hired men's kitchen chambers all his life. Later on Miss Salome came in to see if he was comfortable, and stood, with her candle in her hand, looking down very kindly at the thin, shrewd little face on the pillow.

"I hope you'll sleep real well here, Chester," she said. "I had a little boy once who used to sleep here. You – you look like him. Good night."

She bent over him and kissed his forehead. Chester had never been kissed by anyone before, so far as he could remember. Something came up in his throat that felt about as big as a pumpkin. At the same moment he wished he could have told Miss Salome the whole truth about himself. I might tell her in the morning, he thought, as he watched her figure passing out of the little porch chamber.

But on second thought he decided that this would never do. He felt sure she would disapprove of his running away, and would probably insist upon his going straight back to Upton or, at least, informing Aunt Harriet of his whereabouts. No, he could not tell her.

Clemantiny was an early riser, but when she came into the kitchen the next morning the fire was already made and Chester was out in the yard with three of the five cows milked.

"Humph!" said Clemantiny amiably. "New brooms sweep clean."

But she gave him cream with his porridge that morning. Generally, all Miss Salome's hired hands got from Clemantiny was skim milk.

Miss Salome's regular hired man lived in a little house down in the hollow. He soon turned up, and the other two men she had hired for harvest also arrived. Martin, the man, looked Chester over quizzically.

"What do you think you can do, sonny?"

"Anything," said Chester sturdily. "I'm used to work."

"He's right," whispered Clemantiny aside. "He's smart as a steel trap. But just you keep an eye on him all the same, Martin."

Chester soon proved his mettle in the harvest field. In the brisk three weeks that followed, even Clemantiny had to admit that he earned every cent of his wages. His active feet were untiring and his wiry arms could pitch and stook with the best. When the day's work was ended, he brought in wood and water for Clemantiny, helped milk the cows, gathered the eggs, and made on his own responsibility a round of barns and outhouses to make sure that everything was snug and tight for the night.

"Freckles-and-Bones has been well trained somewhere," said Clemantiny again.

It was hardly fair to put the bones in now, for Chester was growing plump and hearty. He had never been so happy in his life. Upton drudgery and that dreadful week in Montrose seemed like a bad dream. Here, in the golden meadows of Mount Hope Farm, he worked with a right good will. The men liked him, and he soon became a favourite with them. Even Clemantiny relented somewhat. To be sure, she continued very grim, and still threw her words at him as if they were so many missiles warranted to strike home. But Chester soon learned that Clemantiny's bark was worse than her bite. She was really very good to him and fed him lavishly. But she declared that this was only to put some flesh on him.

"It offends me to see bones sticking through anybody's skin like that. We aren't used to such objects at Mount Hope Farm, thank goodness. Yes, you may smile, Salome. I like him well enough, and I'll admit that he knows how to make himself useful, but I don't trust him any more than ever I did. He's mighty close about his past life. You can't get any more out of him than juice out of a post. I've tried, and I know."

But it was Miss Salome who had won Chester's whole heart. He had never loved anybody in his hard little life before. He loved her with an almost dog-like devotion. He forgot that he was working to earn money – and make his fortune. He worked to please Miss Salome. She was good and kind and gentle to him, and his starved heart thawed and expanded in the sunshine of her atmosphere. She went to the little porch room every night to kiss him good night. Chester would have been bitterly disappointed if she had failed to go.

She was greatly shocked to find out that he had never said his prayers before going to bed. She insisted on teaching him the simple little one she had used herself when a child. When Chester found that it would please her, he said it every night. There was nothing he would not have done for Miss Salome.

She talked a good deal to him about Johnny and she gave him the jack-knife that Johnny had owned.

"It belonged to a good, manly little boy once," she said, "and now I hope it belongs to another such."

"I ain't very good," said Chester repentantly, "but I'll try to be, Miss Salome – honest, I will."

One day he heard Miss Salome speaking of someone who had run away from home. "A wicked, ungrateful boy," she called him. Chester blushed until his freckles were drowned out in a sea of red, and Clemantiny saw it, of course. When did anything ever escape those merciless black eyes of Clemantiny's?

"Do you think it's always wrong for a fellow to run away, Miss Salome?" he faltered.

"It can't ever be right," said Miss Salome decidedly.

"But if he wasn't treated well – and was jawed at – and not let go to school?" pleaded Chester.

Clemantiny gave Miss Salome a look as of one who would say, You're bat-blind if you can't read between the lines of that; but Miss Salome was placidly unconscious. She was not really thinking of the subject at all, and did not guess that Chester meant anything more than generalities.

"Not even then," she said firmly. "Nothing can justify a boy for running away – especially as Jarvis Colemen did – never even left a word behind him to say where he'd gone. His aunt thought he'd fallen into the river."

"Don't suppose she would have grieved much if he had," said Clemantiny sarcastically, all the while watching Chester, until he felt as if she were boring into his very soul and reading all his past life.

When the harvest season drew to a close, dismay crept into the soul of our hero. Where would he go now? He hated to think of leaving Mount Hope Farm and Miss Salome. He would have been content to stay there and work as hard as he had ever worked at Upton, merely for the roof over his head and the food he ate. The making of a fortune seemed a small thing compared to the privilege of being near Miss Salome.

"But I suppose I must just up and go," he muttered dolefully.

One day Miss Salome had a conference with Clemantiny. At the end of it the latter said, "Do as you please," in the tone she might have used to a spoiled child. "But if you'd take my advice – which you won't and never do – you'd write to somebody in Upton and make inquiries about him first. What he says is all very well and he sticks to it marvellous, and there's no tripping him up. But there's something behind, Salome Whitney – mark my words, there's something behind."

"He looks so like Johnny," said Miss Salome wistfully.

"And I suppose you think that covers a multitude of sins," said Clemantiny contemptuously.

ON THE DAY WHEN the last load of rustling golden sheaves was carried into the big barn and stowed away in the dusty loft, Miss Salome called Chester into the kitchen. Chester's heart sank as he obeyed the summons.

His time was up, and now he was to be paid his wages and sent away. To be sure, Martin had told him that morning that a man in East Hopedale wanted a boy for a spell, and that he, Martin, would see that he got the place if he wanted it. But that did not reconcile him to leaving Mount Hope Farm.

Miss Salome was sitting in her favourite sunny corner of the kitchen and Clemantiny was flying around with double briskness. The latter's thin lips were tightly set, and disapproval was writ large in every flutter of her calico skirts.

"Chester," said Miss Salome kindly, "your time is up today."

Chester nodded. For a moment he felt as he had felt when he left the provision store in Montrose. But he would not let Clemantiny see him cry. Somehow, he would not have minded Miss Salome.

"What are you thinking of doing now?" Miss Salome went on.

"There's a man at East Hopedale wants a boy," said Chester, "and Martin says he thinks I'll suit."

"That is Jonas Smallman," said Miss Salome thoughtfully. "He has the name of being a hard master. It isn't right of me to say so, perhaps. I really don't know much about him. But wouldn't you rather stay here with me for the winter, Chester?"

"Ma'am? Miss Salome?" stammered Chester. He heard Clemantiny give a snort behind him and mutter, "Clean infatuated – clean infatuated," without in the least knowing what she meant.

"We really need a chore boy all the year round," said Miss Salome. "Martin has all he can do with the heavy work. And there are the apples to be picked. If you care to stay, you shall have your board and clothes for doing the odd jobs, and you can go to school all winter. In the spring we will see what need be done then."

If he would care to stay! Chester could have laughed aloud. His eyes were shining with joy as he replied, "Oh, Miss Salome, I'll be so glad to stay! I – I – didn't want to go away. I'll try to do everything you want me to do. I'll work ever so hard."

"Humph!"

This, of course, was from Clemantiny, as she set a pan of apples on the stove with an emphatic thud. "Nobody ever doubted your willingness to work. Pity everything else about you isn't as satisfactory."

"Clemantiny!" said Miss Salome rebukingly. She put her arms about Chester and drew him to her. "Then it is all settled, Chester. You are my boy now, and of course I shall expect you to be a good boy."

If ever a boy was determined to be good, that boy was Chester. That day was the beginning of a new life for him. He began to go to the Hopedale school the next week. Miss Salome gave him all Johnny's old school books and took an eager interest in his studies.

Chester ought to have been very happy, and at first he was; but, as the bright, mellow days of autumn passed by, a shadow came over his happiness. He could not help thinking that he had really deceived Miss Salome, and was deceiving her still – Miss Salome, who had such confidence in him. He was not what he pretended to be. And as for his running away, he felt sure that Miss Salome would view that with horror. As the time passed by and he learned more and more what a high standard of honour and truth she had, he felt more and more ashamed of himself. When she looked at him with her clear, trustful, blue eyes, Chester felt as guilty as if he had systematically deceived her with intent to do harm. He began to wish that he had the courage to tell her the whole truth about himself.

Moreover, he began to think that perhaps he had not done right, after all, in running away from Aunt Harriet. In Miss Salome's code nothing could be right that was underhanded, and Chester was very swiftly coming to look at things through Miss Salome's eyes. He felt sure that Johnny would never have acted as he had, and if

Chester now had one dear ambition on earth, it was to be as good and manly a fellow as Johnny must have been. But he could never be that as long as he kept the truth about himself from Miss Salome.

"That boy has got something on his mind," said the terrible Clemantiny, who, Chester felt convinced, could see through a stone wall.

"Nonsense! What could he have on his mind?" said Miss Salome. But she said it a little anxiously. She, too, had noticed Chester's absent ways and abstracted face.

"Goodness me, I don't know! I don't suppose he has robbed a bank or murdered anybody. But he is worrying over something, as plain as plain."

"He is getting on very well at school," said Miss Salome. "His teacher says so, and he is very eager to learn. I don't know what can be troubling him."

She was fated not to know for a fortnight longer. During that time Chester fought out his struggle with himself, and conquered. He must tell Miss Salome, he decided, with a long sigh. He knew that it would mean going back to Upton and Aunt Harriet and the old, hard life, but he would not sail under false colours any longer.

CHESTER WENT INTO the kitchen one afternoon when he came home from school, with his lips set and his jaws even squarer than usual. Miss Salome was making some of her famous taffy, and Clemantiny was spinning yarn on the big wheel.

"Miss Salome," said Chester desperately, "if you're not too busy, there is something I'd like to tell you."

"What is it?" asked Miss Salome good-humouredly, turning to him with her spoon poised in midair over her granite saucepan.

"It's about myself. I – I – oh, Miss Salome, I didn't tell you the truth about myself! I've got to tell it now. My

135

name isn't Benson – exactly – and I ran away from home.''

"Dear me!" said Miss Salome mildly. She dropped her spoon, handle and all, into the taffy and never noticed it. "Dear me, Chester!"

"I knew it," said Clemantiny triumphantly. "I knew it – and I always said it. Run away, did you?"

"Yes'm. My name is Chester Benson Stephens, and I lived at Upton with Aunt Harriet Elwell. But she ain't any relation to me, really. She's only father's stepsister. She – she – wasn't kind to me and she wouldn't let me go to school – so I ran away."

"But, dear me, Chester, didn't you know that was very wrong?" said Miss Salome in bewilderment.

"No'm – I didn't know it then. I've been thinking lately that maybe it was. I'm – I'm real sorry."

"What did you say your real name was?" demanded Clemantiny.

"Stephens, ma'am."

"And your mother's name before she was married?"

"Mary Morrow," said Chester, wondering what upon earth Clemantiny meant.

Clemantiny turned to Miss Salome with an air of surrendering a dearly cherished opinion.

"Well, ma'am, I guess you must be right about his looking like Johnny. I must say I never could see the resemblance, but it may well be there, for he – that very fellow there – and Johnny are first cousins. Their mothers were sisters!"

"Clemantiny!" exclaimed Miss Salome.

"You may well say 'Clemantiny.' Such a coincidence! It doesn't make you and him any relation, of course – the cousinship is on the mother's side. But it's there. Mary Morrow was born and brought up in Hopedale. She went to Upton when I did, and married Oliver Stephens there. Why, I knew his father as well as I know you."

"This is wonderful," said Miss Salome. Then she added sorrowfully, "But it doesn't make your running away right, Chester."

"Tell us all about it," demanded Clemantiny, sitting down on the wood-box. "Sit down, boy, sit down – don't stand there looking as if you were on trial for your life. Tell us all about it."

Thus adjured, Chester sat down and told them all about it – his moonlight flitting and his adventures in Montrose. Miss Salome exclaimed with horror over the fact of his sleeping in a pile of lumber for seven nights, but Clemantiny listened in silence, never taking her eyes from the boy's pale face. When Chester finished, she nodded.

"We've got it all now. There's nothing more behind, Salome. It would have been better for you to have told as straight a story at first, young man."

Chester knew that, but, having no reply to make, made none. Miss Salome looked at him wistfully.

"But, with it all, you didn't do right to run away, Chester," she said firmly. "I dare say your aunt was severe with you – but two wrongs never make a right, you know."

"No'm," said Chester.

"You must go back to your aunt," continued Miss Salome sadly.

Chester nodded. He knew this, but he could not trust himself to speak. Then did Clemantiny arise in her righteous indignation.

"Well, I never heard of such nonsense, Salome Whitney! What on earth do you want to send him back for? I knew Harriet Elwell years ago, and if she's still what she was then, it ain't much wonder Chester ran away from her. I'd say 'run,' too. Go back, indeed! You keep him right here, as you should, and let Harriet Elwell look somewhere else for somebody to scold!"

"Clemantiny!" expostulated Miss Salome.

"Oh, I must and will speak my mind, Salome. There's no one else to take Chester's part, it seems. You have as much claim on him as Harriet Elwell has. She ain't any real relation to him any more than you are."

Miss Salome looked troubled. Perhaps there was something in Clemantiny's argument. And she hated to think of seeing Chester go. He looked more like Johnny than ever, as he stood there with his flushed face and wistful eyes.

"Chester," she said gravely, "I leave it to you to decide. If you think you ought to go back to your aunt, well and good. If not, you shall stay here."

This was the hardest yet. Chester wished she had not left the decision to him. It was like cutting off his own hand. But he spoke up manfully.

"I – I think I ought to go back, Miss Salome, and I want to pay back the money, too."

"I think so, too, Chester, although I'm sorry as sorry can be. I'll go back to Upton with you. We'll start tomorrow. If, when we get there, your aunt is willing to let you stay with me, you can come back."

"There's a big chance of that!" said Clemantiny sourly. "A woman's likely to give up a boy like Chester – a good, steady worker and as respectful and obliging as there is between this and sunset – very likely, isn't she! Well, this taffy is all burnt to the saucepan and clean ruined – but what's the odds! All I hope, Salome Whitney, is that the next time you adopt a boy and let him twine himself 'round a person's heart, you'll make sure first that you are going to stick to it. I don't like having my affections torn up by the roots."

Clemantiny seized the saucepan and disappeared with it into the pantry amid a whirl of pungent smoke.

Mount Hope Farm was a strangely dismal place that night. Miss Salome sighed heavily and often as she made her preparations for the morrow's journey.

Clemantiny stalked about with her grim face grimmer than ever. As for Chester, when he went to bed that night in the little porch chamber, he cried heartily into his pillows. He didn't care for pride any longer; he just cried and didn't even pretend he wasn't crying when Miss Salome came in to sit by him a little while and talk to him. That talk comforted Chester. He realized that, come what might, he would always have a good friend in Miss Salome – aye, and in Clemantiny, too.

Chester never knew it, but after he had fallen asleep, with the tears still glistening on his brown cheeks, Clemantiny tiptoed silently in with a candle in her hand and bent over him with an expression of almost maternal tenderness on her face. It was late and an aroma of boiling sugar hung about her. She had sat up long after Miss Salome was abed, to boil another saucepan of taffy for Chester to eat on his journey.

"Poor, dear child!" she said, softly touching one of his crisp curls. "It's a shame in Salome to insist on his going back. She doesn't know what she's sending him to, or she wouldn't. He didn't say much against his aunt, and Salome thinks she was only just a little bit cranky. But *I* could guess."

Early in the morning Miss Salome and Chester started. They were to drive to Montrose, leave their team there and take the boat for Belltown. Chester bade farewell to the porch chamber and the long, white kitchen and the friendly barns with a full heart. When he climbed into the wagon, Clemantiny put a big bagful of taffy into his hands.

"Good-by, Chester," she said. "And remember, you've always got a friend in me, anyhow."

Then Clemantiny went back into the kitchen and cried – good, rough-spoken, tender-hearted Clemantiny sat down and cried.

It was an ideal day for travelling – crisp, clear and sunny – but neither Chester nor Miss Salome was in a mood for enjoyment.

Back over Chester's runaway route they went, and reached Belltown on the boat that evening.

They stayed in Belltown overnight and in the morning took the train to Roxbury Station. Here Miss Salome hired a team from the storekeeper and drove out to Upton.

Chester felt his heart sink as they drove into the Elwell yard. How well he knew it!

Miss Salome tied her hired nag to the gatepost and took Chester by the hand. They went to the door and knocked. It was opened with a jerk and Mrs. Elwell stood before them. She had probably seen them from the window, for she uttered no word of surprise at seeing Chester again. Indeed, she said nothing at all, but only stood rigidly before them.

Dear me, what a disagreeable-looking woman! thought Miss Salome. But she said courteously, "Are you Mrs. Elwell?"

"I am," said that lady forbiddingly.

"I've brought your nephew home," continued Miss Salome, laying her hand encouragingly on Chester's shrinking shoulder. "I have had him hired for some time on my farm at Hopedale, but I didn't know until yesterday that he had run away from you. When he told me about it, I thought he ought to come straight back and return your four dollars, and so did he. So I have brought him."

"You might have saved yourself the trouble then!" cried Mrs. Elwell shrilly. Her black eyes flashed with anger. "I'm done with him and don't want the money. Run away when there was work to do, and thinks he can come back now that it's all done and loaf all winter, does he? He shall never enter my house again."

"That he shall not!" cried Miss Salome, at last finding her tongue. Her gentle nature was grievously stirred by the heartlessness shown in the face and voice of Mrs. Elwell. "That he shall not!" she cried again. "But he shall not want for a home as long as I have one to give him. Come, Chester, we'll go home."

"I wish you well of him," Mrs. Elwell said sarcastically.

Miss Salome already repented her angry retort. She was afraid she had been undignified, but she wished for a moment that Clemantiny was there. Wicked as she feared it was, Miss Salome thought she could have enjoyed a tilt between her ancient handmaid and Mrs. Elwell.

"I beg your pardon, Mrs. Elwell, if I have used any intemperate expressions," she said with great dignity. "You provoked me more than was becoming by your remarks. I wish you good morning."

Mrs. Elwell slammed the door shut.

With her cheeks even more than usually rosy, Miss Salome led Chester down to the gate, untied her horse and drove out of the yard. Not until they reached the main road did she trust herself to speak to the dazed lad beside her.

"What a disagreeable women!" she ejaculated at last. "I don't wonder you ran away, Chester – I don't, indeed! Though, mind you, I don't think it was right, for all that. But I'm gladder than words can say that she wouldn't take you back. You are mine now, and you will stay mine.

I want you to call me Aunt Salome after this. Get up, horse! If we can catch that train at Roxbury, we'll be home by night yet."

Chester was too happy to speak. He had never felt so glad and grateful in his life before.

They got home that night just as the sun was setting redly behind the great maples on the western hill. As they drove into the yard, Clemantiny's face appeared, gazing at them over the high board fence of the cow-yard. Chester waved his hand at her gleefully.

"Lawful heart!" said Clemantiny. She set down her pail and came out to the lane on a run. She caught Chester as he sprang from the wagon and gave him a hearty hug.

"I'm glad clean down to my boot soles to see you back again," she said.

"He's back for good," said Miss Salome. "Chester, you'd better go in and study up your lessons for tomorrow."

Millicent's Double

" ' NONSENSE,' SAID MILLI-
CENT, POINTING TO THEIR
REFLECTED FACES "

HEN MILLICENT MOORE and Worth Gordon met each other on the first day of the term in the entrance hall of the Kinglake High School, both girls stopped short, startled. Millicent Moore had never seen Worth Gordon before, but Worth Gordon's face she had seen every day of her life, looking at her out of her own mirror!

They were total strangers, but when two girls look enough alike to be twins, it is not necessary to stand on ceremony. After the first blank stare of amazement, both laughed outright. Millicent held out her hand.

"We ought to know each other right away," she said frankly. "My name is Millicent Moore, and yours is – ?"

"Worth Gordon," responded Worth, taking the proffered hand with dancing eyes. "You actually frightened me when you came around that corner. For a moment I had an uncanny feeling that I was a disembodied spirit looking at my own outward shape. I know now what it feels like to have a twin."

"Isn't it odd that we should look so much alike?" said Millicent. "Do you suppose we can be any relation? I never heard of any relations named Gordon."

Worth shook her head. "I'm quite sure we're not," she said. "I haven't any relatives except my father's stepsister with whom I've lived ever since the death of my parents when I was a baby."

"Well, you'll really have to count me as a relative after this," laughed Millicent. "I'm sure a girl who looks as much like you as I do must be at least as much relation as a stepaunt."

From that moment they were firm friends, and their friendship was still further cemented by the fact that Worth found it necessary to change her boarding-house and became Millicent's roommate. Their odd likeness

145

was the wonder of the school and occasioned no end of amusing mistakes, for all the students found it hard to distinguish between them. Seen apart it was impossible to tell which was which except by their clothes and style of hairdressing. Seen together there were, of course, many minor differences which served to distinguish them. Both girls were slight, with dark-brown hair, blue eyes and fair complexions. But Millicent had more colour than Worth. Even in repose, Millicent's face expressed mirth and fun; when Worth was not laughing or talking, her face was rather serious. Worth's eyes were darker, and her nose in profile slightly more aquiline. But still, the resemblance between them was very striking. In disposition they were also very similar. Both were merry, fun-loving girls, fond of larks and jokes. Millicent was the more heedless, but both were impulsive and too apt to do or say anything that came into their heads without counting the cost. One late October evening Millicent came in, her cheeks crimson after her walk in the keen autumn air, and tossed two letters on the study table. "It's a perfect evening, Worth. We had the jolliest tramp. You should have come with us instead of staying in moping over your books."

Worth smiled ruefully. "I simply had to prepare those problems for tomorrow," she said. "You see, Millie dear, there is a big difference between us in some things at least. I'm poor. I simply have to pass my exams and get a teacher's licence. So I can't afford to take any chances. You're just attending high school for the sake of education alone, so you don't really have to grind as I do."

"I'd like to do pretty well in the exams, though, for Dad's sake," answered Millicent, throwing aside her wraps. "But I don't mean to kill myself studying, just the same. Time enough for that when exams draw nigh. They're comfortably far off yet. But I'm in a bit of a predicament, Worth, and I don't know what to do. Here are two invitations for Saturday afternoon and I simply *must* accept them both. Now, how can I do it? You're a marvel at mathematics – so work out that problem for me.

"See, here's a note from Mrs. Kirby inviting me to tea at Beechwood. She called on me soon after the term opened and invited me to tea the next week. But I had another engagement for that afternoon, so couldn't go. Mr. Kirby is a business friend of Dad's, and they are very nice people. The other invitation is to the annual autumn picnic of the Alpha Gammas. Now, Worth Gordon, I simply *must* go to that. I wouldn't miss it for anything. But I don't want to offend Mrs. Kirby, and I'm afraid I shall if I plead another engagement a second time. Mother will be fearfully annoyed at me in that case. Dear me, I wish there were two of me, one to go to the Alpha Gammas and one to Beechwood – Worth Gordon!"

"What's the matter?"

"There *are* two of me! What's the use of a double if not for a quandary like this! Worth, you must go to tea at Beechwood Saturday afternoon in my place. They'll think you are my very self. They'll never know the difference. Go and keep my place warm for me, there's a dear."

"Impossible," cried Worth. "I'd never dare! They'd know there was something wrong."

"They wouldn't – they couldn't. None of the Kirbys have ever seen me except Mrs. Kirby, and she only for a few minutes one evening at dusk. They don't know I have a double and they can't possibly suspect. *Do* go, Worth. Why, it'll be a regular lark, the best little joke ever! And you'll oblige me immensely besides. Worthie, *please*."

Worth did not consent all at once; but the idea rather appealed to her for its daring and excitement. It would be a lark – just at that time Worth did not see it in any other light. Besides, she wanted to oblige Millicent, who coaxed vehemently. Finally, Worth yielded and promised Millicent that she would go to Beechwood in her place.

"You darling!" said Millicent emphatically, flying to her table to write acceptances of both invitations.

Saturday afternoon Worth got ready to keep Millicent's engagement. "Suppose I am found out and expelled from Beechwood in disgrace," she suggested laughingly, as she arranged her lace bertha before the glass.

"Nonsense," said Millicent, pointing to their reflected faces. "The Kirbys can never suspect. Why, if it weren't for the hair and the dresses, I'd hardly know myself which of those reflections belonged to which."

"What if they begin asking me about the welfare of the various members of your family?"

"They won't ask any but the most superficial questions. We're not intimate enough for anything else. I've coached you pretty thoroughly, and I think you'll get on all right."

Worth's courage carried her successfully through the ordeal of arriving at Beechwood and meeting Mrs. Kirby. She was unsuspectingly accepted as Millicent Moore, and found her impersonation of that young lady not at all difficult. No dangerous subject of conversation was introduced and nothing personal was said until Mr. Kirby came in. He looked so scrutinizingly at Worth as he shook hands with her that the latter felt her heart beating very fast. Did he suspect?

"Upon my word, Miss Moore," he said genially, "you gave me quite a start at first. You are very like what a half-sister of mine used to be when a girl long ago. Of course the resemblance must be quite accidental."

"Of course," said Worth, without any very clear sense of what she was saying. Her face was uncomfortably flushed and she was glad when tea was announced.

As nothing more of an embarrassing nature was said,

Worth soon recovered her self-possession and was able to enter into the conversation. She liked the Kirbys; still, under her enjoyment, she was conscious of a strange, disagreeable feeling that deepened as the evening wore on. It was not fear – she was not at all afraid of betraying herself now. It had even been easier than she had expected. Then what was it? Suddenly Worth flushed again. She knew now – it was shame. She was a guest in that house as an impostor! What she had done seemed no longer a mere joke. What would her host and hostess say if they knew? That they would never know made no difference. *She* herself could not forget it, and her realization of the baseness of the deception grew stronger under Mrs. Kirby's cordial kindness.

Worth never forgot that evening. She compelled herself to chat as brightly as possible, but under it all was that miserable consciousness of falsehood, deepening every instant. She was thankful when the time came to leave. "You must come up often, Miss Moore," said Mrs. Kirby kindly. "Look upon Beechwood as a second home while you are in Kinglake. We have no daughter of our own, so we make a hobby of cultivating other people's."

When Millicent returned home from the Alpha Gamma outing, she found Worth in their room, looking soberly at the mirror. Something in her chum's expression alarmed her. "Worth, what is it? Did they suspect?"

"No," said Worth slowly. "They never suspected. They think I am what I pretended to be – Millicent Moore. But, but, I wish I'd never gone to Beechwood, Millie. It wasn't right. It was mean and wrong. It was acting a lie. I can't tell you how ashamed I felt when I realized that."

"Nonsense," said Millicent, looking rather sober, nevertheless. "No harm was done. It's only a good joke, Worth."

"Yes, harm *has* been done. I've done harm to myself, for one thing. I've lost my self-respect. I don't blame you,

Millie. It's all my own fault. I've done a dishonourable thing, dishonourable."

Millicent sighed. "The Alpha Gamma picnic was horribly slow," she said. "I didn't enjoy myself a bit. I wish I had gone to Beechwood. I didn't think about it's being a practical falsehood before. I suppose it was. And I've always prided myself on my strict truthfulness! It wasn't your fault, Worth! It was mine. But it can't be undone now."

"No, it can't be undone," said Worth slowly, "but it might be confessed. We might tell Mrs. Kirby the truth and ask her to forgive us."

"I couldn't do such a thing," cried Millicent. "It isn't to be thought of!"

Nevertheless, Millicent did think of it several times that night and all through the following Sunday. She couldn't help thinking of it. A dishonourable trick! That thought stung Millicent. Monday evening Millicent flung down the book from which she was vainly trying to study.

"Worthie, it's no use. You were right. There's nothing to do but go and 'fess up to Mrs. Kirby. I can't respect Millicent Moore again until I do. I'm going right up now."

"I'll go with you," said Worth quietly. "I was equally to blame and I must take my share of the humiliation."

When the girls reached Beechwood, they were shown into the library where the family were sitting. Mrs. Kirby came smilingly forward to greet Millicent when her eyes fell upon Worth. "Why! why!" she said. "I didn't know you had a twin sister, Miss Moore."

"Neither I have," said Millicent, laughing nervously. "This is my chum, Worth Gordon, but she is no relation whatever."

At the mention of Worth's name, Mr. Kirby started slightly, but nobody noticed it. Millicent went on in a trembling voice. "We've come up to confess something,

Mrs. Kirby. I'm sure you'll think it dreadful, but we didn't mean any harm. We just didn't realize, until afterwards."

Then Millicent, with burning cheeks, told the whole story and asked to be forgiven. "I, too, must apologize," said Worth, when Millicent had finished. "Can you pardon me, Mrs. Kirby?"

Mrs. Kirby had listened in amazed silence, but now she laughed. "Certainly," she said kindly. "I don't suppose it was altogether right for you girls to play such a trick on anybody. But I can make allowances for schoolgirl pranks. I was a school girl once myself, and far from a model one. You have atoned for your mistake by coming so frankly and confessing, and now we'll forget all about it. I think you have learned your lesson. Both of you must just sit down and spend the evening with us. Dear me, but you *are* bewilderingly alike!"

"I've something I want to say," interposed Mr. Kirby suddenly. "You say your name is Worth Gordon," he added, turning to Worth. "May I ask what your mother's name was?"

"Worth Mowbray," answered Worth wonderingly.

"I was sure of it," said Mr. Kirby triumphantly, "when I heard Miss Moore mention your name. Your mother was my half-sister, and you are my niece."

Everybody exclaimed and for a few moments they all talked and questioned together. Then Mr. Kirby explained fully. "I was born on a farm up-country. My mother was a widow when she married my father, and she had one daughter, Worth Mowbray, five years older than myself. When I was three years old, my mother died. Worth went to live with our mother's only living relative, an aunt. My father and I removed to another section of the country. He, too, died soon after, and I was brought up with an uncle's family. My sister came to see me once when she was a girl of seventeen and, as I remember her, very like you are now. I never saw her again and eventually lost trace of her. Many years later I endeavoured to find out her whereabouts. Our aunt was dead, and the people in the village where she had lived informed me that my sister was also dead. She had married a man named Gordon and had gone away, both she and her husband had died, and I was informed that they left no children, so I made no further inquiries. There is no doubt that you are her daughter. Well, well, this is a pleasant surprise, to find a little niece in this fashion!"

It was a pleasant surprise to Worth, too, who had thought herself all alone in the world and had felt her loneliness keenly. They had a wonderful evening, talking and questioning and explaining. Mr. Kirby declared that Worth must come and live with them. "We have no daughter," he said. "You must come to us in the place of one, Worth."

Mrs. Kirby seconded this with a cordiality that won Worth's affection at once. The girl felt almost bewildered by her happiness.

"I feel as if I were in a dream," she said to Millicent as they walked to their boarding-house. "It's really all too wonderful to grasp at once. You don't know, Millie, how lonely I've felt often under all my nonsense and fun. Aunt Delia was kind to me, but she was really no relation, she had a large family of her own, and I have always felt that she looked upon me as a rather inconvenient duty. But now I'm so happy!"

"I'm so glad for you, Worth," said Millicent warmly, "although your gain will certainly be my loss, for I shall miss my roommate terribly when she goes to live at Beechwood. Hasn't it all turned out strangely? If you had never gone to Beechwood in my place, this would never have happened."

"Say rather that if we hadn't gone to confess our fault,

it would never have happened," said Worth gently. "I'm very, very glad that I have found Uncle George and such a loving welcome to his home. But I'm gladder still that I've got my self-respect back. I feel that I can look Worth Gordon in the face again."

"I've learned a wholesome lesson, too," admitted Millicent.

Penelope's
Party Waist

"T'S PERFECTLY HORRID to be so poor," grumbled Penelope. Penelope did not often grumble, but just now, as she sat tapping with one pink-tipped finger her invitation to Blanche Anderson's party, she felt that grumbling was the only relief she had.

Penelope was seventeen, and when one is seventeen and cannot go to a party because one hasn't a suitable dress to wear, the world is very apt to seem a howling wilderness.

"I wish I could think of some way to get you a new waist," said Doris, with what these sisters called "the poverty pucker" coming in the centre of her pretty forehead. "If your black skirt were sponged and pressed and re-hung, it would do very well."

Penelope saw the poverty pucker and immediately repented with all her impetuous heart having grumbled. That pucker came often enough without being brought there by extra worries.

"Well, there is no use sitting here sighing for the unattainable," she said, jumping up briskly. "I'd better be putting my grey matter into that algebra instead of wasting it plotting for a party dress that I certainly can't get. It's a sad thing for a body to lack brains when she wants to be a teacher, isn't it? If I could only absorb algebra and history as I can music, what a blessing it would be! Come now, Dorrie dear, smooth that pucker out. Next year I shall be earning a princely salary, which we can squander on party gowns at will – if people haven't given up inviting us by that time, in sheer despair of ever being able to conquer our exclusiveness."

Penelope went off to her detested algebra with a laugh, but the pucker did not go out of Doris' forehead. She wanted Penelope to go to that party.

Penelope has studied so hard all winter and she hasn't

gone anywhere, thought the older sister wistfully. She is getting discouraged over those examinations and she needs just a good, jolly time to hearten her up. If it could only be managed!

But Doris did not see how it could. It took every cent of her small salary as typewriter in an uptown office to run their tiny establishment and keep Penelope in school dresses and books. Indeed, she could not have done even that much if they had not owned their little cottage. Next year it would be easier if Penelope got through her examinations successfully, but just now there was absolutely not a spare penny.

"It is hard to be poor. We are a pair of misfits," said Doris, with a patient little smile, thinking of Penelope's uncultivated talent for music and her own housewifely gifts, which had small chance of flowering out in her business life.

Doris dreamed of pretty dresses all that night and thought about them all the next day. So, it must be confessed, did Penelope, though she would not have admitted it for the world.

When Doris reached home the next evening, she found Penelope hovering over a bulky parcel on the sitting-room table.

"I'm so glad you've come," she said with an exaggerated gasp of relief. "I really don't think my curiosity could have borne the strain for another five minutes. The expressman brought this parcel an hour ago, and there's a letter for you from Aunt Adella on the clock shelf, and I think they belong to each other. Hurry up and find out. Dorrie, darling, what if it should be a – a – present of some sort or other!"

"I suppose it can't be anything else," smiled Doris. She knew that Penelope had started out to say "a new dress."

She cut the strings and removed the wrappings. Both girls stared.

"Is it – it isn't – yes, it is! Doris Hunter, I believe it's an old quilt!"

Doris unfolded the odd present with a queer feeling of disappointment. She did not know just what she had expected the package to contain, but certainly not this. She laughed a little shakily.

"Well, we can't say after this that Aunt Adella never gave us anything," she said, when she had opened her letter. "Listen, Penelope."

My Dear Doris:

I have decided to give up housekeeping and go out West to live with Robert. So I am disposing of such of the family heirlooms as I do not wish to take with me. I am sending you by express your Grandmother Hunter's silk quilt. It is a handsome article still and I hope you will prize it as you should. It took your grandmother five years to make it. There is a bit of the wedding dress of every member of the family in it. Love to Penelope and yourself.

Your affectionate aunt,
Adella Hunter.

"I don't see its beauty," said Penelope with a grimace. "It may have been pretty once, but it is all faded now. It is a monument of patience, though. The pattern is what they call 'Little Thousands,' isn't it? Tell me, Dorrie, does it argue a lack of proper respect for my ancestors that I can't feel very enthusiastic over this heirloom – especially when Grandmother Hunter died years before I was born?"

"It was very kind of Aunt Adella to send it," said Doris dutifully.

"Oh, very," agreed Penelope drolly. "Only don't ever

ask me to sleep under it. It would give me the nightmare. O – o – h!"

This last was a little squeal of admiration as Doris turned the quilt over and brought to view the shimmering lining.

"Why, the wrong side is ever so much prettier than the right!" exclaimed Penelope. "What lovely, old-timey stuff! And not a bit faded."

The lining was certainly very pretty. It was a soft, creamy yellow silk, with a design of brocaded pink rose-buds all over it.

"That was a dress Grandmother Hunter had when she was a girl," said Doris absently. "I remember hearing Aunt Adella speak of it. When it became old-fashioned, Grandmother used it to line her quilt. I declare, it is as good as new."

"Well, let us go and have tea," said Penelope. "I'm decidedly hungry. Besides, I see the poverty pucker coming. Put the quilt in the spare room. It is something to possess an heirloom, after all. It gives one a nice, important-family feeling."

After tea, when Penelope was patiently grinding away at her studies and thinking dolefully enough of the near-approaching examinations, which she dreaded, and of teaching, which she confidently expected to hate, Doris went up to the tiny spare room to look at the wrong side of the quilt again.

"It would make the loveliest party waist," she said under her breath. "Creamy yellow is Penelope's colour, and I could use that bit of old black lace and those knots of velvet ribbon that I have to trim it. I wonder if Grandmother Hunter's reproachful spirit will forever haunt me if I do it."

Doris knew very well that she would do it – had known

it ever since she had looked at that lovely lining and a vision of Penelope's vivid face and red-brown hair rising above a waist of the quaint old silk had flashed before her mental sight. That night, after Penelope had gone to bed, Doris ripped the lining out of Grandmother Hunter's silk quilt.

"If Aunt Adella saw me now!" she laughed softly to herself as she worked.

In the three following evenings Doris made the waist. She thought it a wonderful bit of good luck that Penelope went out each of the evenings to study some especially difficult problems with a school chum.

"It will be such a nice surprise for her," the sister mused jubilantly.

Penelope was surprised as much as the tender, sisterly heart could wish when Doris flashed out upon her triumphantly on the evening of the party with the black skirt nicely pressed and re-hung, and the prettiest waist imaginable – a waist that was a positive "creation" of dainty rose-besprinkled silk, with a girdle and knots of black velvet.

"Doris Hunter, you are a veritable little witch! Do you mean to tell me that you conjured that perfectly lovely thing for me out of the lining of Grandmother Hunter's quilt?"

So Penelope went to Blanche's party and her dress was the admiration of every girl there. Mrs. Fairweather, who was visiting Mrs. Anderson, looked closely at it also. She was a very sweet old lady, with silver hair, which she wore in delightful, old-fashioned puffs, and she had very bright, dark eyes. Penelope thought her altogether charming.

"She looks as if she had just stepped out of the frame of some lovely old picture," she said to herself. "I wish she belonged to me. I'd just love to have a grandmother like her. And I do wonder who it is I've seen who looks so much like her."

A little later on the knowledge came to her suddenly, and she thought with inward surprise: Why, it is Doris, of course. If my sister Doris lives to be seventy years old and wears her hair in pretty white puffs, she will look exactly as Mrs. Fairweather does now.

Mrs. Fairweather asked to have Penelope introduced to her, and when they found themselves alone together she said gently, "My dear, I am going to ask a very impertinent question. Will you tell me where you got the silk of which your waist is made?"

Poor Penelope's pretty young face turned crimson. She was not troubled with false pride by any means, but she simply could not bring herself to tell Mrs. Fairweather that her waist was made out of the lining of an old heirloom quilt.

"My Aunt Adella gave me – gave us – the material," she stammered. "And my elder sister Doris made the waist for me. I think the silk once belonged to my Grandmother Hunter."

"What was your grandmother's maiden name?" asked Mrs. Fairweather eagerly.

"Penelope Saverne. I am named after her."

Mrs. Fairweather suddenly put her arm about Penelope and drew the young girl to her, her lovely old face aglow with delight and tenderness.

"Then you are my grandniece," she said. "Your grandmother was my half-sister. When I saw your dress, I felt sure you were related to her. I should recognize that rosebud silk if I came across it in Thibet. Penelope Saverne was the daughter of my mother by her first husband. Penelope was four years older than I was, but we were devoted to each other. Oddly enough, our birthdays fell on the same day, and when Penelope was twenty and I sixteen, my father gave us each a silk dress of this very material. I have mine yet.

"Soon after this our mother died and our household was broken up. Penelope went to live with her aunt and I went West with Father. This was long ago, you know, when travelling and correspondence were not the easy, matter-of-course things they are now. After a few years I lost touch with my half-sister. I married out West and have lived there all my life. I never knew what had become of Penelope. But tonight, when I saw you come in in that waist made of the rosebud silk, the whole past rose before me and I felt like a girl again. My dear, I am a very lonely old woman, with nobody belonging to me. You don't know how delighted I am to find that I have two grandnieces."

Penelope had listened silently, like a girl in a dream. Now she patted Mrs. Fairweather's soft old hand affectionately.

"It sounds like a storybook," she said gaily. "You must come and see Doris. She is such a darling sister. I wouldn't have had this waist if it hadn't been for her. I will tell you the whole truth – I don't mind it now. Doris made my party waist for me out of the lining of an old silk quilt of Grandmother Hunter's that Aunt Adella sent us."

Mrs. Fairweather did go to see Doris the very next day, and quite wonderful things came to pass from that interview. Doris and Penelope found their lives and plans changed in the twinkling of an eye. They were both to go and live with Aunt Esther – as Mrs. Fairweather had said they must call her. Penelope was to have, at last, her longed-for musical education and Doris was to be the home girl.

"You must take the place of my own dear little grand-daughter," said Aunt Esther. "She died six years ago, and I have been so lonely since."

When Mrs. Fairweather had gone, Doris and Penelope looked at each other.

"Pinch me, please," said Penelope. "I'm half afraid I'll wake up and find I have been dreaming. Isn't it all wonderful, Doris Hunter?"

Doris nodded radiantly.

"Oh, Penelope, think of it! Music for you – somebody to pet and fuss over for me – and such a dear, sweet aunty for us both!"

"And no more contriving party waists out of old silk linings," laughed Penelope. "But it was very fortunate that you did it for once, sister mine. And no more poverty puckers," she concluded.

The Little
Black Doll

VERYBODY IN the Marshall household was excited on the evening of the concert at the Harbour Light Hotel – everybody, even to Little Joyce, who couldn't go to the concert because there wasn't anybody else to stay with Denise. Perhaps Denise was the most excited of them all – Denise, who was slowly dying of consumption in the Marshall kitchen chamber because there was no other place in the world for her to die in, or anybody to trouble about her. Mrs. Roderick Marshall thought it very good of herself to do so much for Denise. To be sure, Denise was not much bother, and Little Joyce did most of the waiting on her.

At the tea table nothing was talked of but the concert; for was not Madame Laurin, the great French Canadian prima donna, at the hotel, and was she not going to sing? It was the opportunity of a lifetime – the Marshalls would not have missed it for anything. Stately, handsome old Grandmother Marshall was going, and Uncle Roderick and Aunt Isabella, and of course Chrissie, who was always taken everywhere because she was pretty and graceful, and everything that Little Joyce was not.

Little Joyce would have liked to go to the concert, for she was very fond of music; and, besides, she wanted to be able to tell Denise all about it. But when you are shy and homely and thin and awkward, your grandmother never takes you anywhere. At least, such was Little Joyce's belief.

Little Joyce knew quite well that Grandmother Marshall did not like her. She thought it was because she was so plain and awkward – and in part it was. Grandmother Marshall cared very little for granddaughters who did not do her credit. But Little Joyce's mother had married a poor man in the face of her family's disapproval, and then both she and her husband had been inconsiderate enough to die and leave a small orphan without a penny to support her. Grandmother Marshall fed and clothed the child, but who could make anything of such a shy creature with no gifts or graces whatever? Grandmother Marshall had no intention of trying. Chrissie, the golden-haired and pink-cheeked, was Grandmother Marshall's pet.

Little Joyce knew this. She did not envy Chrissie but, oh, how she wished Grandmother Marshall would love her a little, too! Nobody loved her but Denise and the little black doll. And Little Joyce was beginning to understand that Denise would not be in the kitchen chamber very much longer, and the little black doll couldn't *tell* you she loved you – although she did, of course. Little Joyce had no doubt at all on this point.

Little Joyce sighed so deeply over this thought that Uncle Roderick smiled at her. Uncle Roderick *did* smile at her sometimes.

"What is the matter, Little Joyce?" he asked.

"I was thinking about my black doll," said Little Joyce timidly.

"Ah, your black doll. If Madame Laurin were to see it, she'd likely want it. She makes a hobby of collecting dolls all over the world, but I doubt if she has in her collection a doll that served to amuse a little girl four thousand years ago in the court of the Pharaohs."

"I think Joyce's black doll is very ugly," said Chrissie. "My wax doll with the yellow hair is ever so much prettier."

"My black doll isn't ugly," cried Little Joyce indignantly. She could endure to be called ugly herself, but she could not bear to have her darling black doll called ugly. In her excitement she upset her cup of tea over the tablecloth. Aunt Isabella looked angry, and Grandmother Marshall said sharply: "Joyce, leave the table. You grow more awkward and careless every day."

Little Joyce, on the verge of tears, crept away and went up the kitchen stairs to Denise to be comforted. But Denise herself had been crying. She lay on her little bed by the low window, where the glow of the sunset was coming in; her hollow cheeks were scarlet with fever.

"Oh! I want so much to hear Madame Laurin sing," she sobbed. "I feel lak I could die easier if I hear her sing just one leetle song. She is Frenchwoman, too, and she sing all de ole French songs – de ole songs my mudder sing long 'go. Oh! I so want to hear Madame Laurin sing."

"But you can't, dear Denise," said Little Joyce very softly, stroking Denise's hot forehead with her cool, slender hand. Little Joyce had very pretty hands, only nobody had ever noticed them. "You are not strong enough to go to the concert. I'll sing for you, if you like. Of course, I can't sing very well, but I'll do my best."

"You sing lak a sweet bird, but you are not Madame Laurin," said Denise restlessly. "It is de great Madame I want to hear. I haf not long to live. Oh, I know, Leetle Joyce – I know what de doctor look lak – and I want to hear Madame Laurin sing 'fore I die. I know it is impossible – but I long for it so – just one leetle song."

Denise put her thin hands over her face and sobbed again. Little Joyce went and sat down by the window, looking out into the white birches. Her heart ached bitterly. Dear Denise was going to die soon – oh, very soon! Little Joyce, wise and knowing beyond her years, saw that. And Denise wanted to hear Madame Laurin sing. It seemed a foolish thing to think of, but Little Joyce thought hard about it; and when she had finished thinking, she got her little black doll and took it to bed with her, and there she cried herself to sleep.

AKIN TO ANNE

At the breakfast table next morning the Marshalls talked about the concert and the wonderful Madame Laurin. Little Joyce listened in her usual silence; her crying the night before had not improved her looks any. Never, thought handsome Grandmother Marshall, had she appeared so sallow and homely. Really, Grandmother Marshall could not have the patience to look at her. She decided that she would not take Joyce driving with her and Chrissie that afternoon, as she had thought of, after all.

In the forenoon it was discovered that Denise was much worse, and the doctor was sent for. He came, and shook his head, that being really all he could do under the circumstances. When he went away, he was waylaid at the back door by a small gypsy with big, black, serious eyes and long black hair.

"Is Denise going to die?" Little Joyce asked in the blunt, straightforward fashion Grandmother Marshall found so trying.

The doctor looked at her from under his shaggy brows and decided that here was one of the people to whom you might as well tell the truth first as last, because they are bound to have it.

"Yes," he said.

"Soon?"

"Very soon, I'm afraid. In a few days at most."

"Thank you," said Little Joyce gravely.

She went to her room and did something with the black doll. She did not cry, but if you could have seen her face you would have wished she would cry.

After dinner Grandmother Marshall and Chrissie drove away, and Uncle Roderick and Aunt Isabella went away, too. Little Joyce crept up to the kitchen chamber. Denise was lying in an uneasy sleep, with tear stains on her face.

Then Little Joyce tiptoed down and sped away to the hotel.

She did not know just what she would say or do when she got there, but she thought hard all the way to the end of the shore road. When she came out to the shore, a lady was sitting alone on a big rock – a lady with a dark, beautiful face and wonderful eyes. Little Joyce stopped before her and looked at her meditatively. Perhaps it would be well to ask advice of this lady.

"If you please," said Little Joyce, who was never shy with strangers, for whose opinion she didn't care at all, "I want to see Madame Laurin at the hotel and ask her to do me a very great favour. Will you tell me the best way to go about seeing her? I shall be much obliged to you."

"What is the favour you want to ask of Madame Laurin?" inquired the lady, smiling.

"I want to ask her if she will come and sing for Denise before she dies – before Denise dies, I mean. Denise is our French girl, and the doctor says she cannot live very long, and she wishes with all her heart to hear Madame Laurin sing. It is very bitter, you know, to be dying and want something very much and not be able to get it."

"Do you think Madame Laurin will go?" asked the lady.

"I don't know. I am going to offer her my little black doll. If she will not come for that, there is nothing else I can do."

A flash of interest lighted up the lady's brown eyes. She bent forward.

"Is it your doll you have in that box? Will you let me see it?"

Little Joyce nodded. Mutely she opened the box and took out the black doll. The lady gave an exclamation of amazed delight and almost snatched it from Little Joyce.

It was a very peculiar little doll indeed, carved out of some black polished wood.

"Child, where in the world did you get this?" she cried.

"Father got it out of a grave in Egypt," said Little Joyce. "It was buried with the mummy of a little girl who lived four thousand years ago, Uncle Roderick says. She must have loved her doll very much to have had it buried with her, mustn't she? But she could not have loved it any more than I do."

"And yet you are going to give it away?" said the lady, looking at her keenly.

"For Denise's sake," explained Little Joyce. "I would do anything for Denise because I love her and she loves me. When the only person in the world who loves you is going to die, there is nothing you would not do for her if you could. Denise was so good to me before she took sick. She used to kiss me and play with me and make little cakes for me and tell me beautiful stories."

The lady put the little black doll back in the box. Then she stood up and held out her hand.

"Come," she said. "I am Madame Laurin, and I shall go and sing for Denise."

Little Joyce piloted Madame Laurin home and into the kitchen and up the back stairs to the kitchen chamber – a proceeding which would have filled Aunt Isabella with horror if she had known. But Madame Laurin did not seem to mind, and Little Joyce never thought about it at all. It was Little Joyce's awkward, unMarshall-like fashion to go to a place by the shortest way there, even if it was up the kitchen stairs.

Madame Laurin stood in the bare little room and looked pityingly at the wasted, wistful face on the pillow.

"This is Madame Laurin, and she is going to sing for you, Denise," whispered Little Joyce.

Denise's face lighted up, and she clasped her hands.

"If you please," she said faintly. "A French song, Madame – de ole French song dey sing long 'go."

Then did Madame Laurin sing. Never had that kitchen chamber been so filled with glorious melody. Song after song she sang – the old folklore songs of the *habitant*, the songs perhaps that Evangeline listened to in her childhood.

Little Joyce knelt by the bed, her eyes on the singer like one entranced. Denise lay with her face full of joy and rapture – such joy and rapture! Little Joyce did not regret the sacrifice of her black doll – never could regret it, as long as she remembered Denise's look.

"T'ank you, Madame," said Denise brokenly, when Madame ceased. "Dat was so beautiful – de angel, dey cannot sing more sweet. I love music so much, Madame. Leetle Joyce, she sing to me often and often – she sing sweet, but not lak you – oh, not lak you."

"Little Joyce must sing for me," said Madame, smiling, as she sat down by the window. "I always like to hear fresh, childish voices. Will you, Little Joyce?"

"Oh, yes." Little Joyce was quite unembarrassed and perfectly willing to do anything she could for this wonderful woman who had brought that look to Denise's face. "I will sing as well as I can for you. Of course, I can't sing very well and I don't know anything but hymns. I always sing hymns for Denise, although she is a Catholic and the hymns are Protestant. But her priest told her it was all right, because all music was of God. Denise's priest is a very nice man, and I like him. He thought my little black doll – *your* little black doll – was splendid. I'll sing 'Lead, Kindly Light.' That is Denise's favourite hymn."

Then Little Joyce, slipping her hand into Denise's, began to sing. At the first note Madame Laurin, who had been gazing out of the window with a rather listless smile, turned quickly and looked at Little Joyce with amazed eyes. Delight followed amazement, and when Little Joyce had finished, the great Madame rose impulsively, her face and eyes glowing, stepped swiftly to Little Joyce and took the thin dark face between her gemmed hands.

"Child, do you know what a wonderful voice you have – what a marvellous voice? It is – it is – I never heard such a voice in a child of your age. Mine was nothing to it – nothing at all. You will be a great singer some day – far greater than I – yes. But you must have the training. Where are your parents? I must see them."

"I have no parents," said the bewildered Little Joyce. "I belong to Grandmother Marshall, and she is out driving."

"Then I shall wait until your Grandmother Marshall comes home from her drive," said Madame Laurin decidedly.

Half an hour later a very much surprised old lady was listening to Madame Laurin's enthusiastic statements.

"How is it I have never heard you sing, if you can sing so well?" asked Grandmother Marshall, looking at Little Joyce with something in her eyes that had never been in them before – as Little Joyce instantly felt to the core of her sensitive soul. But Little Joyce hung her head. It had never occurred to her to sing in Grandmother Marshall's presence.

"This child must be trained by-and-by," said Madame Laurin. "If you cannot afford it, Mrs. Marshall, I will see to it. Such a voice must not be wasted."

"Thank you, Madame Laurin," said Grandmother Marshall with a gracious dignity, "but I am quite able to give my granddaughter all the necessary advantages for the development of her gift. And I thank you very much for telling me of it."

Madame Laurin bent and kissed Little Joyce's brown cheek.

"Little gypsy, good-by. But come every day to this hotel to see me. And next summer I shall be back. I like you – because some day you will be a great singer and because today you are a loving, unselfish baby."

"You have forgotten the little black doll, Madame," said Little Joyce gravely.

Madame threw up her hands, laughing. "No, no, I shall not take your little black doll of the four thousand years. Keep it for a mascot. A great singer always needs a mascot. But do not, I command you, take it out of the box till I am gone, for if I were to see it again, I might not be able to resist the temptation. Some day I shall show you *my* dolls, but there is not such a gem among them."

When Madame Laurin had gone, Grandmother Marshall looked at Little Joyce.

"Come to my room, Joyce. I want to see if we cannot find a more becoming way of arranging your hair. It has grown so thick and long. I had no idea how thick and long. Yes, we must certainly find a better way than that stiff braid. Come!"

Little Joyce, taking Grandmother Marshall's extended hand, felt very happy. She realized that this strange, stately old lady, who never liked little girls unless they were pretty or graceful or clever, was beginning to love her at last.

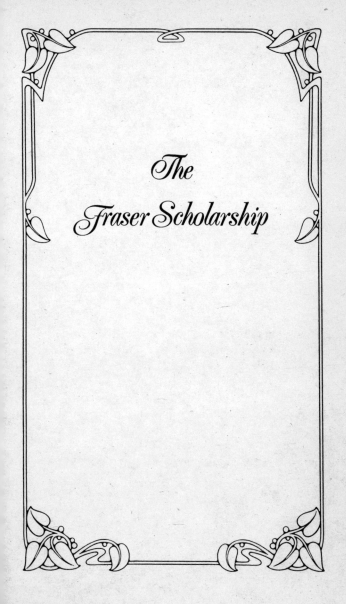

The

Fraser Scholarship

LLIOTT CAMPBELL came down the main staircase of Marwood College and found himself caught up with a whoop into a crowd of Sophs who were struggling around the bulletin board. He was thumped on the back and shaken hands with amid a hurricane of shouts and congratulations.

"Good for you, Campbell! You've won the Fraser. See your little name tacked up there at the top of the list, bracketed off all by itself for the winner? 'Elliott H. Campbell, ninety-two per cent.' A class yell for Campbell, boys!"

While the yell was being given with a heartiness that might have endangered the roof, Elliott, with flushed face and sparkling eyes, pushed nearer to the important type-written announcement on the bulletin board. Yes, he had won the Fraser Scholarship. His name headed the list of seven competitors.

Roger Brooks, who was at his side, read over the list aloud:

" 'Elliott H. Campbell, ninety-two.' I said you'd do it, my boy. 'Edward Stone, ninety-one' – old Ned ran you close, didn't he? But of course with that name he'd no show. 'Kay Milton, eighty-eight.' Who'd have thought slow-going old Kay would have pulled up so well? 'Seddon Brown, eighty-seven; Oliver Field, eighty-four; Arthur McIntyre, eighty-two' – a very respectable little trio. *And* 'Carl McLean, seventy.' Whew! what a drop! Just saved his distance. It was only his name took him in, of course. He knew you weren't supposed to be strong in mathematics."

Before Elliott could say anything, a professor emerged from the president's private room, bearing the report of a Freshman examination, which he proceeded to post on the Freshman bulletin board, and the rush of the students in that direction left Elliott and Roger free of the crowd. They seized the opportunity to escape.

Elliott drew a long breath as they crossed the campus in the fresh April sunshine, where the buds were swelling on the fine old chestnuts and elms that surrounded Marwood's red brick walls.

"That has lifted a great weight off my mind," he said frankly. "A good deal depended on my winning the Fraser. I couldn't have come back next year if I hadn't got it. That four hundred will put me through the rest of my course."

"That's good," said Roger Brooks heartily.

He liked Elliott Campbell, and so did all the Sophomores. Yet none of them was at all intimate with him. He had no chums, as the other boys had. He boarded alone, "dug" persistently, and took no part in the social life of the college. Roger Brooks came nearest to being his friend of any, yet even Roger knew very little about him. Elliott had never before said so much about his personal affairs as in the speech just recorded.

"I'm poor – woefully poor," went on Elliott gaily. His success seemed to have thawed his reserve for the time being. "I had just enough money to bring me through the Fresh and Soph years by dint of careful management. Now I'm stone broke, and the hope of the Fraser was all that stood between me and the dismal certainty of having to teach next year, dropping out of my class and coming back in two or three years' time, a complete, rusty stranger again. Whew! I made faces over the prospect."

"No wonder," commented Roger. "The class would have been sorry if you had had to drop out, Campbell. We want to keep all our stars with us to make a shining coruscation at the finish. Besides, you know we all like you for yourself. It would have been an everlasting shame if that little cad of a McLean had won out. Nobody likes him."

"Oh, I had no fear of him," answered Elliott. "I don't see what induced him to go in, anyhow. He must have known he'd no chance. But I was afraid of Stone – he's a born dabster at mathematics, you know, and I only hold my own in them by hard digging."

"Why, Stone couldn't have taken the Fraser over you in any case, if you made over seventy," said Roger with a puzzled look. "You must have known that. McLean was the only competitor you had to fear."

"I don't understand you," said Elliott blankly.

"You must know the conditions of the Fraser!" exclaimed Roger.

"Certainly," responded Elliott. " 'The Fraser scholarship, amounting to four hundred dollars, will be offered annually in the Sophomore class. The competitors will be expected to take a special examination in mathematics, and the winner will be awarded two hundred dollars for two years, payable in four annual instalments, the payment of any instalment to be conditional on the winner's attending the required classes for undergraduates and making satisfactory progress therein.' Isn't that correct?"

"So far as it goes, old man. You forget the most important part of all. 'Preference is to be given to competitors of the name Fraser, Campbell or McLean, provided that such competitor makes at least seventy per cent in his examination.' You don't mean to tell me that you didn't know that!"

"Are you joking?" demanded Elliott with a pale face.

"Not a joke. Why, man, it's in the calendar."

"I didn't know it," said Elliott slowly. "I read the calendar announcement only once, and I certainly didn't notice that condition."

"Well, that's curious. But how on earth did you escape hearing it talked about? It's always discussed extensively among the boys, especially when there are two competitors of the favoured names, which doesn't often happen."

"I'm not a very sociable fellow," said Elliott with a faint smile. "You know they call me 'the hermit.' As it happened, I never talked the matter over with anyone or heard it referred to. I – I wish I had known this before."

"Why, what difference does it make? It's all right, anyway. But it is odd to think that if your name hadn't been Campbell, the Fraser would have gone to McLean over the heads of Stone and all the rest. Their only hope was that you would both fall below seventy. It's an absurd condition, but there it is in old Professor Fraser's will. He was rich and had no family. So he left a number of bequests to the college on ordinary conditions. I suppose he thought he might humour his whim in one. His widow is a dear old soul, and always makes a special pet of the boy who wins the Fraser. Well, here's my street. So long, Campbell."

Elliott responded almost curtly and walked onward to his boarding-house with a face from which all the light had gone. When he reached his room he took down the Marwood calendar and whirled over the leaves until he came to the announcement of bursaries and scholarships. The Fraser announcement, as far as he had read it, ended at the foot of the page. He turned the leaf and, sure enough, at the top of the next page, in a paragraph by itself, was the condition: "Preference shall be given to candidates of the name Fraser, Campbell or McLean, provided that said competitor makes at least seventy per cent in his examination."

Elliott flung himself into a chair by his table and bowed his head on his hands. He had no right to the

Fraser Scholarship. His name was not Campbell, although perhaps nobody in the world knew it save himself, and he remembered it only by an effort of memory.

He had been born in a rough mining camp in British Columbia, and when he was a month old his father, John Hanselpakker, had been killed in a mine explosion, leaving his wife and child quite penniless and almost friendless. One of the miners, an honest, kindly Scotchman named Alexander Campbell, had befriended Mrs. Hanselpakker and her little son in many ways, and two years later she had married him. They returned to their native province of Nova Scotia and settled in a small country village. Here Elliott had grown up, bearing the name of the man who was a kind and loving father to him, and whom he loved as a father. His mother had died when he was ten years old and his stepfather when he was fifteen. On his deathbed he asked Elliott to retain his name.

"I've cared for you and loved you since the time you were born, lad," he said. "You seem like my own son, and I've a fancy to leave you my name. It's all I can leave you, for I'm a poor man, but it's an honest name, lad, and I've kept it free from stain. See that you do likewise, and you'll have your mother's blessing and mine."

Elliott fought a hard battle that spring evening.

"Hold your tongue and keep the Fraser," whispered the tempter. "Campbell *is* your name. You've borne it all your life. And the condition itself is a ridiculous one – no fairness about it. You made the highest marks and you ought to be the winner. It isn't as if you were wronging Stone or any of the others who worked hard and made good marks. If you throw away what you've won by your own hard labour, the Fraser goes to McLean, who made only seventy. Besides, you need the money and he doesn't. His father is a rich man."

"But I'll be a cheat and a cad if I keep it," Elliott muttered miserably. "Campbell isn't my legal name, and I'd never again feel as if I had even the right of love to it if I stained it by a dishonest act. For it *would* be stained, even though nobody but myself knew it. Father said it was a clean name when he left it, and I cannot soil it."

The tempter was not silenced so easily as that. Elliott passed a sleepless night of indecision. But next day he went to Marwood and asked for a private interview with the president. As a result, an official announcement was posted that afternoon on the bulletin board to the effect that, owing to a misunderstanding, the Fraser Scholarship had been wrongly awarded. Carl McLean was posted as winner.

The story soon got around the campus, and Elliott found himself rather overwhelmed with sympathy, but he did not feel as if he were very much in need of it after all. It was good to have done the right thing and be able to look your conscience in the face. He was young and strong and could work his own way through Marwood in time.

"No condolences, please," he said to Roger Brooks with a smile. "I'm sorry I lost the Fraser, of course, but I've my hands and brains left. I'm going straight to my boarding-house to dig with double vim, for I've got to take an examination next week for a provincial school certificate. Next winter I'll be a flourishing pedagogue in some up-country district."

He was not, however. The next afternoon he received a summons to the president's office. The president was there, and with him was a plump, motherly-looking woman of about sixty.

"Mrs. Fraser, this is Elliott Hanselpakker, or Campbell, as I understand he prefers to be called. Elliott, I told your story to Mrs. Fraser last evening, and she was greatly

184

interested when she heard your rather peculiar name. She will tell you why herself."

"I had a young half-sister once," said Mrs. Fraser eagerly. "She married a man named John Hanselpakker and went West, and somehow I lost all trace of her. There was, I regret to say, a coolness between us over her marriage. I disapproved of it because she married a very poor man. When I heard your name, it struck me that you might be her son, or at least know something about her. Her name was Mary Helen Rodney, and I loved her very dearly in spite of our foolish quarrel."

There was a tremour in Mrs. Fraser's voice and an answering one in Elliott's as he replied: "Mary Helen Rodney was my dear mother's name, and my father was John Hanselpakker."

"Then you are my nephew," exclaimed Mrs. Fraser. "I am your Aunt Alice. My boy, you don't know how much it means to a lonely old woman to have found you. I'm the happiest person in the world!"

She slipped her arm through Elliott's and turned to the sympathetic president with shining eyes.

"He is my boy forever, if he will be. Blessings on the Fraser Scholarship!"

"Blessings rather on the manly boy who wouldn't keep it under false colours," said the president with a smile. "I think you are fortunate in your nephew, Mrs. Fraser."

So Elliott Hanselpakker Campbell came back to Marwood the next year after all.

Her Own People

HE TAUNTON SCHOOL had closed for the summer holidays. Constance Foster and Miss Channing went down the long, elm-shaded street together, as they generally did, because they happened to board on the same block downtown.

Constance was the youngest teacher on the staff, and had charge of the Primary Department. She had taught in Taunton school a year, and at its close she was as much of a stranger in the little corps of teachers as she had been at the beginning. The others thought her stiff and unapproachable; she was unpopular in a negative way with all except Miss Channing, who made it a profession to like everybody, the more so if other people disliked them. Miss Channing was the oldest teacher on the staff, and taught the fifth grade. She was short and stout and jolly; nothing, not even the iciest reserve, ever daunted Miss Channing.

"Isn't it good to think of two whole blessed months of freedom?" she said jubilantly. "Two months to dream, to be lazy, to go where one pleases, no exercises to correct, no reports to make, no pupils to keep in order. To be sure, I love them every one, but I'll love them all the more for a bit of a rest from them. Isn't it good?"

A little satirical smile crossed Constance Foster's dark, discontented face, looking just then all the more discontented in contrast to Miss Channing's rosy, beaming countenance.

"It's very good, if you have anywhere to go, or anybody who cares where you go," she said bitterly. "For my own part, I'm sorry school is closed. I'd rather go on teaching all summer."

"Heresy!" said Miss Channing. "Rank heresy! What are your vacation plans?"

"I haven't any," said Constance wearily. "I've put off

thinking about vacation as long as I possibly could. You'll call that heresy, too, Miss Channing."

"It's worse than heresy," said Miss Channing briskly. "It's a crying necessity for blue pills, that's what it is. Your whole mental and moral and physical and spiritual system must be out of kilter, my child. No vacation plans! You *must* have vacation plans. You must be going *somewhere*."

"Oh, I suppose I'll hunt up a boarding place somewhere in the country, and go there and mope until September."

"Have you no friends, Constance?"

"No – no, I haven't anybody in the world. That is why I hate vacation, that is why I've hated to hear you and the others discussing your vacation plans. You all have somebody to go to. It has just filled me up with hatred of my life."

Miss Channing swallowed her honest horror at such a state of feeling.

"Constance, tell me about yourself. I've often wanted to ask you, but I was always a little afraid to. You seem so reserved and – and, as if you didn't want to be asked about yourself."

"I know it. I know I'm stiff and hateful, and that nobody likes me, and that it is all my own fault. No, never mind trying to smooth it over, Miss Channing. It's the truth, and it hurts me, but I can't help it. I'm getting more bitter and pessimistic and unwholesome every day of my life. Sometimes it seems as if I hated all the world because I'm so lonely in it. I'm nobody. My mother died when I was born – and Father – oh, I don't know. One can't say anything against one's father, Miss Channing. But I had a hard childhood – or rather, I didn't have any childhood at all. We were always moving about. We didn't seem to have any friends at all. My mother might have had relatives somewhere, but I never heard of any. I don't even know where her home was. Father never would talk of her. He died two years ago, and since then I've been absolutely alone."

"Oh, you poor girl," said Miss Channing softly.

"I want friends," went on Constance, seeming to take a pleasure in open confession now that her tongue was loosed. "I've always just longed for somebody belonging to me to love. I don't love anybody, Miss Channing, and when a girl is in that state, she is all wrong. She gets hard and bitter and resentful – I have, anyway. I struggled against it at first, but it has been too much for me. It poisons everything. There is nobody to care anything about me, whether I live or die."

"Oh, yes, there is One," said Miss Channing gently. "God cares, Constance."

Constance gave a disagreeable little laugh.

"That sounds like Miss Williams – she is so religious. God doesn't mean anything to me, Miss Channing. I've just the same resentful feeling toward him that I have for all the world, if he exists at all. There, I've shocked you in good earnest now. You should have left me alone, Miss Channing."

"God means nothing to you because you've never had him translated to you through human love, Constance," said Miss Channing seriously. "No, you haven't shocked me – at least, not in the way you mean. I'm only terribly sorry."

"Oh, never mind me," said Constance, freezing up into her reserve again as if she regretted her confidences. "I'll get along all right. This is one of my off days, when everything looks black."

Miss Channing walked on in silence. She must help Constance, but Constance was not easily helped. When school reopened, she might be able to do something worthwhile for the girl, but just now the only thing to do was to put her in the way of a pleasant vacation.

"You spoke of boarding," she said, when Constance paused at the door of her boarding-house. "Have you any particular place in view? No? Well, I know a place which I am sure you would like. I was there two summers ago. It is a country place about a hundred miles from here. Pine Valley is its name. It's restful and homey, and the people are so nice. If you like, I'll give you the address of the family I boarded with."

"Thank you," said Constance indifferently. "I might as well go there as anywhere else."

"Yes, but listen to me, dear. Don't take your morbidness with you. Open your heart to the summer, and let its sunshine in, and when you come back in the fall, come prepared to let us all be your friends. We'd like to be, and while friendship doesn't take the place of the love of one's own people, still it is a good and beautiful thing. Besides, there are other unhappy people in the world – try to help them when you meet them, and you'll forget about yourself. Good-by for now, and I hope you'll have a pleasant vacation in spite of yourself."

Constance went to Pine Valley, but she took her evil spirit with her. Not even the beauty of the valley, with its great balmy pines, and the cheerful friendliness of its people could exorcise it.

Nevertheless, she liked the place and found a wholesome pleasure in the long tramps she took along the piney roads.

"I saw such a pretty spot in my ramble this afternoon," she told her landlady one evening. "It is about three miles from here at the end of the valley. Such a picturesque, low-eaved little house, all covered over with honeysuckle. It was set between a big orchard and an old-fashioned flower garden with great pines at the back."

"Heartsease Farm," said Mrs. Hewitt promptly. "Bless you, there's only one place around here of that description. Mr. and Mrs. Bruce, Uncle Charles and Aunt Flora, as we all call them, live there. They are the dearest old couple alive. You ought to go and see them, they'd be delighted. Aunt Flora just loves company. They're real lonesome by times."

"Haven't they any children?" asked Constance indifferently. Her interest was in the place, not in the people.

"No. They had a niece once, though. They brought her up and they just worshipped her. She ran away with a worthless fellow – I forget his name, if I ever knew it. He was handsome and smooth-tongued, but he was a scamp. She died soon after and it just broke their hearts. They don't even know where she was buried, and they never heard anything more about her husband. I've heard that Aunt Flora's hair turned snow-white in a month. I'll take you up to see her some day when I find time."

Mrs. Hewitt did not find time, but thereafter Constance ordered her rambles that she might frequently pass Heartsease Farm. The quaint old spot had a strange attraction for her. She found herself learning to love it, and so unused was this unfortunate girl to loving anything that she laughed at herself for her foolishness.

One evening a fortnight later Constance, with her arms full of ferns and wood-lilies, came out of the pine woods above Heartsease Farm just as heavy raindrops began to fall. She had prolonged her ramble unseasonably, and it was now nearly night, and very certainly a rainy night at that. She was three miles from home and without even an extra wrap.

She hurried down the lane, but by the time she

reached the main road, the few drops had become a downpour. She must seek shelter somewhere, and Hearts-ease Farm was the nearest. She pushed open the gate and ran up the slope of the yard between the hedges of sweetbriar. She was spared the trouble of knocking, for as she came to a breathless halt on the big red sandstone doorstep, the door was flung open, and the white-haired, happy-faced little woman standing on the threshold had seized her hand and drawn her in bodily before she could speak a word.

"I saw you coming from upstairs," said Aunt Flora glee-fully, "and I just ran down as fast as I could. Dear, dear, you are a little wet. But we'll soon dry you. Come right in – I've a bit of a fire in the grate, for the evening is chilly. They laughed at me for loving a fire so, but there's noth-ing like its snap and sparkle. You're rained in for the night, and I'm as glad as I can be. I know who you are – you are Miss Foster. I'm Aunt Flora, and this is Uncle Charles."

Constance let herself be put into a cushiony chair and fussed over with an unaccustomed sense of pleasure. The rain was coming down in torrents, and she certainly was domiciled at Heartsease Farm for the night. Some-how, she felt glad of it. Mrs. Hewitt was right in calling Aunt Flora sweet, and Uncle Charles was a big, jolly, ruddy-faced old man with a hearty manner. He shook Constance's hand until it ached, threw more pine knots in the fire and told her he wished it would rain every night if it rained down a nice little girl like her.

She found herself strangely attracted to the old couple. The name of their farm was in perfect keeping with their atmosphere. Constance's frozen soul expanded in it. She chatted merrily and girlishly, feeling as if she had known them all her life.

When bedtime came, Aunt Flora took her upstairs to a little gable room.

"My spare room is all in disorder just now, dearie, we have been painting its floor. So I'm going to put you here in Jeannie's room. Someway you remind me of her, and you are just about the age she was when she left us. If it wasn't for that, I don't think I could put you in her room, not even if every other floor in the house were being painted. It is so sacred to me. I keep it just as she left it, not a thing is changed. Good night, dearie, and I hope you'll have pleasant dreams."

When Constance found herself alone in the room, she looked about her with curiosity. It was a very dainty, old-fashioned little room. The floor was covered with braided mats; the two square, small-paned windows were draped with snowy muslin. In one corner was a little white bed with white curtains and daintily ruffled pillows, and in the other a dressing table with a gilt-framed mirror and the various knick-knacks of a girlish toilet. There was a little blue rocker and an ottoman with a work-basket on it. In the work-basket was a bit of unfinished, yellowed lace with a needle sticking in it. A small bookcase under the sloping ceiling was filled with books.

Constance picked up one and opened it at the yellowing title-page. She gave a little cry of surprise. The name written across the page in a fine, dainty script was "Jean Constance Irving," her mother's name!

For a moment Constance stood motionless. Then she turned impulsively and hurried downstairs again. Mr. and Mrs. Bruce were still in the sitting room talking to each other in the firelight.

"Oh," cried Constance excitedly. "I must know, I must ask you. This is my mother's name, Jean Constance Irving, can it be possible she was your little Jeannie?"

A FORTNIGHT LATER Miss Channing received a letter from Constance.

"I am so happy," she wrote. "Oh, Miss Channing, I have found 'mine own people,' and Heartsease Farm is to be my own, own dear home for always.

"It was such a strange coincidence, no, Aunt Flora says it was Providence, and I believe it was, too. I came here one rainy night, and Aunty put me in my mother's room, think of it! My own dear mother's room, and I found her name in a book. And now the mystery is all cleared up, and we are so happy.

"Everything is dear and beautiful, and almost the dearest and most beautiful thing is that I am getting acquainted with my mother, the mother I never knew before. She no longer seems dead to me. I feel that she lives and loves me, and I am learning to know her better every day. I have her room and her books and all her little girlish possessions. When I read her books, with their passages underlined by her hand, I feel as if she were speaking to me. She was very good and sweet, in spite of her one foolish, bitter mistake, and I want to be as much like her as I can.

"I said that this was *almost* the dearest and most beautiful thing. The very dearest and most beautiful is this – God means something to me now. He means so much! I remember that you said to me that he meant nothing to me because I had no human love in my heart to translate the divine. But I have now, and it has led me to Him.

"I am not going back to Taunton. I have sent in my resignation. I am going to stay home with Aunty and Uncle. It is so sweet to say *home* and know what it means.

"Aunty says you must come and spend all your next vacation with us. You see, I have lots of vacation plans

now, even for a year ahead. After all, there is no need of
the blue pills!

"I feel like a new creature, made over from the heart
and soul out. I look back with shame and contrition on
the old Constance. I want you to forget her and only
remember your grateful friend, the *new* Constance."

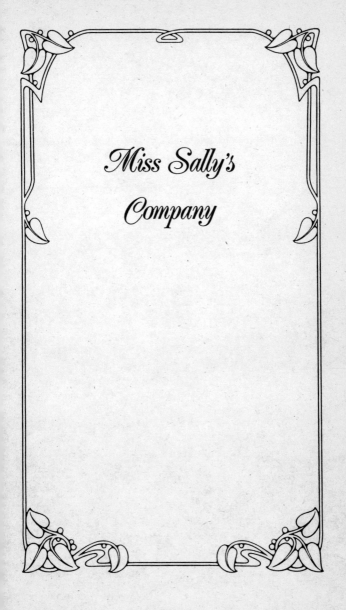

Miss Sally's

Company

"OW BEAUTIFUL!" said Mary Seymour delightedly, as they dismounted from their wheels on the crest of the hill. "Ida, who could have supposed that such a view would be our reward for climbing that long, tedious hill with its ruts and stones? Don't you feel repaid?"

"Yes, but I am dreadfully thirsty," said Ida, who was always practical and never as enthusiastic over anything as Mary was. Yet she, too, felt a keen pleasure in the beauty of the scene before them. Almost at their feet lay the sea, creaming and shimmering in the mellow sunshine. Beyond, on either hand, stretched rugged brown cliffs and rocks, here running out to sea in misty purple headlands, there curving into bays and coves that seemed filled up with sunlight and glamour and pearly hazes; a beautiful shore and, seemingly, a lonely one. The only house visible from where the girls stood was a tiny grey one, with odd, low eaves and big chimneys, that stood down in the little valley on their right, where the cliffs broke away to let a brook run out to sea and formed a small cove, on whose sandy shore the waves lapped and crooned within a stone's throw of the house. On either side of the cove a headland made out to sea, curving around to enclose the sparkling water as in a cup.

"What a picturesque spot!" said Mary.

"But what a lonely one!" protested Ida. "Why, there isn't another house in sight. I wonder who lives in it. Anyway, I'm going down to ask them for a drink of water."

"I'd like to ask for a square meal, too," said Mary, laughing. "I am discovering that I am hungry. Fine scenery is very satisfying to the soul, to be sure, but it doesn't still the cravings of the inner girl. And we've wheeled ten miles this afternoon. I'm getting hungrier every minute."

They reached the little grey house by way of a sloping, grassy lane. Everything about it was very neat and trim. In front a white-washed paling shut in the garden which, sheltered as it was by the house, was ablaze with poppies and hollyhocks and geraniums. A path, bordered by big white clam shells, led through it to the front door, whose steps were slabs of smooth red sandstone from the beach.

"No children here, certainly," whispered Ida. "Every one of those clam shells is placed just so. And this walk is swept every day. No, we shall never dare to ask for anything to eat here. They would be afraid of our scattering crumbs."

Ida lifted her hand to knock, but before she could do so, the door was thrown open and a breathless little lady appeared on the threshold.

She was very small, with an eager, delicately featured face and dark eyes twinkling behind gold-rimmed glasses. She was dressed immaculately in an old-fashioned gown of grey silk with a white muslin fichu crossed over her shoulders, and her silvery hair fell on each side of her face in long, smooth curls that just touched her shoulders and bobbed and fluttered with her every motion; behind, it was caught up in a knot on her head and surmounted by a tiny lace cap.

She looks as if she had just stepped out of a bandbox of last century, thought Mary.

"Are you Cousin Abner's girls?" demanded the little lady eagerly. There was such excitement and expectation in her face and voice that both the Seymour girls felt uncomfortably that they ought to be "Cousin Abner's girls."

"No," said Mary reluctantly, "we're not. We are only – Martin Seymour's girls."

All the light went out of the little lady's face, as if some

202

illuminating lamp had suddenly been quenched behind it. She seemed fairly to droop under her disappointment. As for the rest, the name of Martin Seymour evidently conveyed no especial meaning to her ears. How could she know that he was a multi-millionaire who was popularly supposed to breakfast on railroads and lunch on small corporations, and that his daughters were girls whom all people delighted to honour?

"No, of course you are not Cousin Abner's girls," she said sorrowfully. "I'd have known you couldn't be if I had just stopped to think. Because you are dark and they would be fair, of course; Cousin Abner and his wife were both fair. But when I saw you coming down the lane – I was peeking through the hall window upstairs, you know, I and Juliana – I was sure you were Helen and Beatrice at last. And I can't help wishing you were!"

"I wish we were, too, since you expected them," said Mary, smiling. "But –"

"Oh, I wasn't really expecting them," broke in the little lady. "Only I am always hoping that they will come. They never have yet, but Trenton isn't so very far away, and it is so lonely here. I just long for company – I and Juliana – and I thought I was going to have it today. Cousin Abner came to see me once since I moved here and he said the girls would come, too, but that was six months ago and they haven't come yet. But perhaps they will soon. It is always something to look forward to, you know."

She talked in a sweet, chirpy voice like a bird's. There were pathetic notes in it, too, as the girls instinctively felt. How very quaint and sweet and unworldly she was! Mary found herself feeling indignant at Cousin Abner's girls, whoever they were, for their neglect.

"We are out for a spin on our wheels," said Ida, "and we are very thirsty. We thought perhaps you would be kind enough to give us a drink of water."

"Oh, my dear, anything – anything I have is at your service," said the little lady delightedly. "If you will come in, I will get you some lemonade."

"I am afraid it is too much trouble," began Mary.

"Oh, no, no," cried the little lady. "It is a pleasure. I love doing things for people, I wish more of them would come to give me the chance. I never have any company, and I do so long for it. It's very lonesome here at Golden Gate. Oh, if you would only stay to tea with me, it would make me so happy. I am all prepared. I prepare every Saturday morning, in particular, so that if Cousin Abner's girls did come, I would be all ready. And when nobody comes, Juliana and I have to eat everything up ourselves. And that is bad for us – it gives Juliana indigestion. If you would only stay!"

"We will," agreed Ida promptly. "And we're glad of the chance. We are both terribly hungry, and it is very good of you to ask us."

"Oh, indeed, it isn't! It's just selfishness in me, that's what it is, pure selfishness! I want company so much. Come in, my dears, and I suppose I must introduce myself because you don't know me, do you now? I'm Miss Sally Temple, and this is Golden Gate Cottage. Dear me, this *is* something like living. You are special providences, that you are, indeed!"

She whisked them through a quaint little parlour, where everything was as dainty and neat and old-fashioned as herself, and into a spare bedroom beyond it, to put off their hats.

"Now, just excuse me a minute while I run out and tell Juliana that we are going to have company to tea. She will be so glad, Juliana will. Make yourselves at home, my dears."

"Isn't she delicious?" said Mary, when Miss Sally had

tripped out. "I'd like to shake Cousin Abner's girls. This is what Dot Halliday would call an adventure, Ida."

"Isn't it! Miss Sally and this quaint old spot both seem like a chapter out of the novels our grandmothers cried over. Look here, Mary, she is lonely and our visit seems like a treat to her. Let us try to make it one. Let's just chum with her and tell her all about ourselves and our amusements and our dresses. That sounds frivolous, but you know what I mean. She'll like it. Let's be company in real earnest for her."

When Miss Sally came back, she was attended by Juliana carrying a tray of lemonade glasses. Juliana proved to be a diminutive lass of about fourteen whose cheerful, freckled face wore an expansive grin of pleasure. Evidently Juliana was as fond of "company" as her mistress was. Afterwards, the girls overheard a subdued colloquy between Miss Sally and Juliana out in the hall.

"Go set the table, Juliana, and put on Grandmother Temple's wedding china – be sure you dust it carefully – and the best tablecloth – and be sure you get the crease straight – and put some sweet peas in the centre – and be sure they are fresh. I want everything extra nice, Juliana."

"Yes'm, Miss Sally, I'll see to it. Isn't it great to have company, Miss Sally?" whispered Juliana.

The Seymour girls long remembered that tea table and the delicacies with which it was heaped. Privately, they did not wonder that Juliana had indigestion when she had to eat many such unaided. Being hungry, they did full justice to Miss Sally's good things, much to that little lady's delight.

She told them all about herself. She had lived at Golden Gate Cottage only a year.

"Before that, I lived away down the country at Millbridge with a cousin. My Uncle Ephraim owned Golden Gate Cottage, and when he died he left it to me and I came here to live. It is a pretty place, isn't it? You see those two headlands out there? In the morning, when the sun rises, the water between them is just a sea of gold, and that is why Uncle Ephraim had a fancy to call his place Golden Gate. I love it here. It is so nice to have a home of my own. I would be quite content if I had more company. But I have you today, and perhaps Beatrice and Helen will come next week. So I've really a great deal to be thankful for."

"What is your Cousin Abner's other name?" asked Mary, with a vague recollection of hearing of Beatrice and Helen – somebody – in Trenton.

"Reed – Abner Abimelech Reed," answered Miss Sally promptly. "A. A. Reed, he signs himself now. He is very well-to-do, I am told, and he carries on business in town. He was a very fine young man, my Cousin Abner. I don't know his wife."

Mary and Ida exchanged glances. Beatrice and Helen Reed! They knew them slightly as the daughters of a new-rich family who were hangers-on of the fashionable society in Trenton. They were regarded as decidedly vulgar, and so far their efforts to gain an entry into the exclusive circle where the Seymours and their like revolved had not been very successful.

"I'm afraid Miss Sally will wait a long while before she sees Cousin Abner's girls," said Mary, when they had gone back to the parlour and Miss Sally had excused herself to superintend the washing of Grandmother Temple's wedding china. "They probably look on her as a poor relation to be ignored altogether; whereas, if they were only like her, Trenton society would have made a place for them long ago."

The Seymour girls enjoyed that visit as much as Miss

Sally did. She was eager to hear all about their girlish lives and amusements. They told her of their travels, of famous men and women they had seen, of parties they had attended, the dresses they wore, the little fads and hobbies of their set – all jumbled up together and all listened to eagerly by Miss Sally and also by Juliana, who was permitted to sit on the stairs out in the hall and so gather in the crumbs of this intellectual feast.

"Oh, you've been such pleasant company," said Miss Sally when the girls went away.

Mary took the little lady's hands in hers and looked affectionately down into her face.

"Would you like it – you and Juliana – if we came out to see you often? And perhaps brought some of our friends with us?"

"Oh, if you only would!" breathed Miss Sally.

Mary laughed and, obeying a sudden impulse, bent and kissed Miss Sally's cheek.

"We'll come then," she promised. "Please look upon us as your 'steady company' henceforth."

The girls kept their word. Thereafter, nearly every Saturday of the summer found them taking tea with Miss Sally at Golden Gate. Sometimes they came alone; sometimes they brought other girls. It soon became a decided "fad" in their set to go to see Miss Sally. Everybody who met her loved her at sight. It was considered a special treat to be taken by the Seymours to Golden Gate.

As for Miss Sally, her cup of happiness was almost full. She had "company" to her heart's content, and of the very kind she loved – bright, merry, fun-loving girls who devoured her dainties with a frank zest that delighted her, filled the quaint old rooms with laughter and life, and chattered to her of all their plans and frolics and hopes. There was just one little cloud on Miss Sally's fair sky.

"If only Cousin Abner's girls would come!" she once said wistfully to Mary. "Nobody can quite take the place of one's own, you know. My heart yearns after them."

Mary was very silent and thoughtful as she drove back to Trenton that night. Two days afterwards, she went to Mrs. Gardiner's lawn party. The Reed girls were there. They were tall, fair, handsome girls, somewhat too lavishly and pronouncedly dressed in expensive gowns and hats, and looking, as they felt, very much on the outside of things. They brightened and bridled, however, when Mrs. Gardiner brought Mary Seymour up and introduced her. If there was one thing on earth that the Reed girls longed for more than another it was to "get in" with the Seymour girls.

After Mary had chatted with them for a few minutes in a friendly way, she said, "I think we have a mutual friend in Miss Sally Temple of Golden Gate, haven't we? I'm sure I've heard her speak of you."

The Reed girls flushed. They did not care to have the rich Seymour girls know of their connection with that queer old cousin of their father's who lived in that out-of-the-world spot up-country.

"She is a distant cousin of ours," said Beatrice carelessly, "but we've never met her."

"Oh, how much you have missed!" said Mary frankly. "She is the sweetest and most charming little lady I have ever met, and I am proud to number her among my friends. Golden Gate is such an idyllic little spot, too. We go there so often that I fear Miss Sally will think we mean to outwear our welcome. We hope to have her visit us in town this winter. Well, good-by for now. I'll tell Miss Sally I've met you. She will be pleased to hear about you."

When Mary had gone, the Reed girls looked at each other.

"I suppose we ought to have gone to see Cousin Sally before," said Beatrice. "Father said we ought to."

"How on earth did the Seymours pick her up?" said Helen. "Of course we must go and see her."

Go they did. The very next day Miss Sally's cup of happiness brimmed right over, for Cousin Abner's girls came to Golden Gate at last. They were very nice to her, too. Indeed, in spite of a good deal of snobbishness and false views of life, they were good-hearted girls under it all; and some plain common sense they had inherited from their father came to the surface and taught them to see that Miss Sally was a relative of whom anyone might be proud. They succumbed to her charm, as the others had done, and thoroughly enjoyed their visit to Golden Gate. They went away promising to come often again; and I may say right here that they kept their promise, and a real friendship grew up between Miss Sally and "Cousin Abner's girls" that was destined to work wonders for the latter, not only socially and mentally but spiritually as well, for it taught them that sincerity and honest kindliness of heart and manner are the best passports everywhere, and that pretence of any kind is a vulgarity not to be tolerated. This took time, of course. The Reed girls could not discard their snobbishness all at once. But in the end it was pretty well taken out of them.

Miss Sally never dreamed of this or the need for it. She loved Cousin Abner's girls from the first and always admired them exceedingly.

"And then it is so good to have your own folks coming as company," she told the Seymour girls. "Oh, I'm just in the seventh heaven of happiness. But, dearies, I think you will always be my favourites – mine and Juliana's. I've plenty of company now and it's all thanks to you."

"Oh, no," said Mary quickly. "Miss Sally, your company comes to you for just your own sake. You've made Golden Gate a veritable Mecca for us all. You don't know and you never will know how much good you have done us. You are so good and true and sweet that we girls all feel as if we were bound to live up to you, don't you see? And we all love you, Miss Sally."

"I'm so glad," breathed Miss Sally with shining eyes, "and so is Juliana."

The Story of
an Invitation

ERTHA SUTHERLAND hurried home from the post office and climbed the stairs of her boarding-house to her room on the third floor. Her roommate, Grace Maxwell, was sitting on the divan by the window, looking out into the twilight.

A year ago Bertha and Grace had come to Dartmouth to attend the Academy, and found themselves room-mates. Bertha was bright, pretty and popular, the favour-ite of her classmates and teachers; Grace was a grave, quiet girl, dressed in mourning. She was quite alone in the world, the aunt who had brought her up having re-cently died. At first she had felt shy with bright and brilliant Bertha; but they soon became friends, and the year that followed was a very pleasant one. It was almost ended now, for the terminal exams had begun, and in a week's time the school would close for the holidays.

"Have some chocolates, Grace," said Bertha gaily. "I got such good news in my letter tonight that I felt I must celebrate it fittingly. So I went into Carter's and invested all my spare cash in caramels. It's really fortunate the term is almost out, for I'm nearly bankrupt. I have just enough left to furnish a 'tuck-out' for commencement night, and no more."

"What is your good news, may I ask?" said Grace.

"You know I have an Aunt Margaret – commonly called Aunt Meg – out at Riversdale, don't you? There never was such a dear, sweet, jolly aunty in the world. I had a letter from her tonight. Listen, I'll read you what she says."

I want you to spend your holidays with me, my dear.
Mary Fairweather and Louise Fyshe and Lily Dennis
are coming, too. So there is just room for one more,
and that one must be yourself. Come to Riversdale
when school closes, and I'll feed you on strawberries
and cream and pound cake and doughnuts and mince

*pies, and all the delicious, indigestible things that
school girls love and careful mothers condemn. Mary
and Lou and Lil are girls after your own heart, I know,
and you shall all do just as you like, and we'll have
picnics and parties and merry doings galore.*

"There," said Bertha, looking up with a laugh. "Isn't
that lovely?"

"How delightful it must be to have friends like that to
love you and plan for you," said Grace wistfully. "I am
sure you will have a pleasant vacation, Bertie. As for me, I
am going into Clarkman's bookstore until school re-
opens. I saw Mr. Clarkman today and he agreed to take
me."

Bertha looked surprised. She had not known what
Grace's vacation plans were.

"I don't think you ought to do that, Grace," she said
thoughtfully. "You are not strong, and you need a good
rest. It will be awfully trying to work at Clarkman's all
summer."

"There is nothing else for me to do," said Grace, trying
to speak cheerfully. "You know I'm as poor as the prover-
bial church mouse, Bertie, and the simple truth is that I
can't afford to pay my board all summer and get my
winter outfit unless I do something to earn it. I shall be
too busy to be lonesome, and I shall expect long, newsy
letters from you, telling me all your fun – passing your
vacation on to me at second-hand, you see. Well, I must
set to work at those algebra problems. I tried them before
dark, but I couldn't solve them. My head ached and I felt
so stupid. How glad I shall be when exams are over."

"I suppose I must revise that senior English this
evening," said Bertha absently.

But she made no move to do so. She was studying her
friend's face. How very pale and thin Grace looked – surely much paler and thinner than when she had come to

214

the Academy, and she had not by any means been plump and rosy then.

I believe she could not stand two months at Clarkman's, thought Bertha. If I were not going to Aunt Meg's, I would ask her to go home with me. Or even if Aunt Meg had room for another guest, I'd just write her all about Grace and ask if I could bring her with me. Aunt Meg would understand – she always understands. But she hasn't, so it can't be.

Just then a thought darted into Bertha's brain.

"What nonsense!" she said aloud so suddenly and forcibly that Grace fairly jumped.

"What is?"

"Oh, nothing much," said Bertha, getting up briskly. "See here, I'm going to get to work. I've wasted enough time."

She curled herself up on the divan and tried to study her senior English. But her thoughts wandered hopelessly, and finally she gave it up in despair and went to bed. There she could not sleep; she lay awake and wrestled with herself. It was after midnight when she sat up in bed and said solemnly, "I will do it."

Next day Bertha wrote a confidential letter to Aunt Meg. She thanked her for her invitation and then told her all about Grace.

"And what I want to ask, Aunt Meg, is that you will let me transfer my invitation to Grace, and ask her to go to Riversdale this summer in my place. Don't think me ungrateful. No, I'm sure you won't, you always understand things. But you can't have us both, and I'd rather Grace should go. It will do her so much good, and I have a lovely home of my own to go to, and she has none."

Aunt Meg understood, as usual, and was perfectly willing. So she wrote to Bertha and enclosed a note of invitation for Grace.

I shall have to manage this affair very carefully, reflected Bertha. Grace must never suspect that I did it on purpose. I will tell her that circumstances have prevented me from accepting Aunt Meg's invitation. That is true enough – no need to say that the circumstances are hers, not mine. And I'll say I just asked Aunt Meg to invite her in my place and that she has done so.

When Grace came home from her history examination that day, Bertha told her story and gave her Aunt Meg's cordial note.

"You must come to me in Bertha's place," wrote the latter. "I feel as if I knew you from her letters, and I will consider you as a sort of honorary niece, and I'll treat you as if you were Bertha herself."

"Isn't it splendid of Aunt Meg?" said Bertha diplomatically. "Of course you'll go, Gracie."

"Oh, I don't know," said Grace in bewilderment. "Are you sure you don't want to go, Bertha?"

"Indeed, I do want to go, dreadfully," said Bertha frankly. "But as I've told you, it is impossible. But if I am disappointed, Aunt Meg musn't be. You must go, Grace, and that is all there is about it."

In the end, Grace did go, a little puzzled and doubtful still, but thankful beyond words to escape the drudgery of the counter and the noise and heat of the city. Bertha went home, feeling a little bit blue in secret, it cannot be denied, but also feeling quite sure that if she had to do it all over again, she would do just the same.

The summer slipped quickly by, and finally two letters came to Bertha, one from Aunt Meg and one from Grace.

"I've had a lovely time," wrote the latter, "and, oh, Bertie, what do you think? I am to stay here always. Oh, of course I am going back to school next month, but this is to be my home after this. Aunt Meg – she makes me call her that – says I must stay with her for good."

In Aunt Meg's letter was this paragraph:
*Grace is writing to you, and will have told you that I
intend to keep her here. You know I have always wanted
a daughter of my own, but my greedy brothers and
sisters would never give me one of theirs. So I intend
to adopt Grace. She is the sweetest girl in the world,
and I am very grateful to you for sending her here. You
will not know her when you see her. She has grown
plump and rosy.*

Bertha folded her letters up with a smile. "I have a
vague, delightful feeling that I am the good angel in a
storybook," she said.

The Softening of
Miss Cynthia

"I WONDER IF I'd better flavour this cake with lemon or vanilla. It's the most perplexing thing I ever heard of in my life."

Miss Cynthia put down the bottles with a vexed frown; her perplexity had nothing whatever to do with flavouring the golden mixture in her cake bowl. Mrs. John Joe knew that; the latter had dropped in in a flurry of curiosity concerning the little boy whom she had seen about Miss Cynthia's place for the last two days. Her daughter Kitty was with her; they both sat close together on the kitchen sofa.

"It *is* too bad," said Mrs. John Joe sympathetically. "I don't wonder you are mixed up. So unexpected, too! When did he come?"

"Tuesday night," said Miss Cynthia. She had decided on the vanilla and was whipping it briskly in. "I saw an express wagon drive into the yard with a boy and a trunk in it and I went out just as he got down. 'Are you my Aunt Cynthia?' he said. 'Who in the world are you?' I asked. And he says, 'I'm Wilbur Merrivale, and my father was John Merrivale. He died three weeks ago and he said I was to come to you, because you were his sister.' Well, you could just have knocked me down with a feather!"

"I'm sure," said Mrs. John Joe. "But I didn't know you had a brother. And his name – Merrivale?"

"Well, he wasn't any relation really. I was about six years old when my father married his mother, the Widow Merrivale. John was just my age, and we were brought up together just like brother and sister. He was a real nice fellow, I must say. But he went out to Californy years ago, and I haven't heard a word of him for fifteen years – didn't know if he was alive or dead. But it seems from what I can make out from the boy, that his mother died when he was a baby, and him and John roughed it along together – pretty poor, too, I guess – till John took a fever and died. And he told some of his friends to send the boy to me, for he'd no relations there and not a cent in the world. And the child came all the way from Californy, and here he is. I've been just distracted ever since. I've never been used to children, and to have the house kept in perpetual uproar is more than I can stand. He's about twelve and a born mischief. He'll tear through the rooms with his dirty feet, and he's smashed one of my blue vases and torn down a curtain and set Towser on the cat half a dozen times already – I never was so worried. I've got him out on the verandah shelling peas now, to keep him quiet for a little spell."

"I'm really sorry for you," said Mrs. John Joe. "But, poor child, I suppose he's never had anyone to look after him. And come all the way from Californy alone, too – he must be real smart."

"Too smart, I guess. He must take after his mother, whoever she was, for there ain't a bit of Merrivale in him. And he's been brought up pretty rough."

"Well, it'll be a great responsibility for you, Cynthia, of course. But he'll be company, too, and he'll be real handy to run errands and –"

"*I'm* not going to keep him," said Miss Cynthia determinedly. Her thin lips set themselves firmly and her voice had a hard ring.

"Not going to keep him?" said Mrs. John Joe blankly. "You can't send him back to Californy!"

"I don't intend to. But as for having him here to worry my life out and keep me in a perpetual stew, I just won't do it. D'ye think I'm going to trouble myself about children at my age? And all he'd cost for clothes and schooling, too! I can't afford it. I don't suppose his father expected it either. I suppose he expected me to look after him a bit – and of course I will. A boy of his age ought to be able to earn his keep, anyway. If I look out a place for him somewhere where he can do odd jobs and go to school in the winter, I think it's all anyone can expect of me, when he ain't really no blood relation."

Miss Cynthia flung the last sentence at Mrs. John Joe rather defiantly, not liking the expression on that lady's face.

"I suppose nobody could expect more, Cynthy," said Mrs. John Joe deprecatingly. "He would be an awful bother, I've no doubt, and you've lived alone so long with no one to worry you that you wouldn't know what to do with him. Boys are always getting into mischief – my four just keep me on the dead jump. Still, it's a pity for him, poor little fellow! No mother or father – it seems hard."

Miss Cynthia's face grew grimmer than ever as she went to the door with her callers and watched them down the garden path. As soon as Mrs. John Joe saw that the door was shut, she unburdened her mind to her daughter.

"Did you ever hear tell of the like? I thought I knew Cynthia Henderson well, if anybody in Wilmot did, but this beats me. Just think, Kitty – there she is, no one knows how rich, and not a soul in the world belonging to her, and she won't even take in her brother's child. She must be a hard woman. But it's just meanness, pure and simple; she grudges him what he'd eat and wear. The poor mite doesn't look as if he'd need much. Cynthia didn't used to be like that, but it's growing on her every day. She's got hard as rocks."

That afternoon Miss Cynthia harnessed her fat grey pony into the phaeton herself – she kept neither man nor maid, but lived in her big, immaculate house in solitary state – and drove away down the dusty, buttercup-bordered road, leaving Wilbur sitting on the verandah. She returned in an hour's time and drove into the yard, shutting the gate behind her with a vigorous snap. Wilbur was not in sight and, fearful lest he should be in mischief, she hurriedly tied the pony to the railing and went in search of him. She found him sitting by the well, his chin in his hands; he was pale and his eyes were red. Miss Cynthia hardened her heart and took him into the house.

"I've been down to see Mr. Robins this afternoon, Wilbur," she said, pretending to brush some invisible dust from the bottom of her nice black cashmere skirt for an excuse to avoid looking at him, "and he's agreed to take you on trial. It's a real good chance – better than you could expect. He says he'll board and clothe you and let you go to school in the winter."

The boy seemed to shrink.

"Daddy said that I would stay with you," he said wistfully. "He said you were so good and kind and would love me for his sake."

For a moment Miss Cynthia softened. She had been very fond of her stepbrother; it seemed that his voice appealed to her across the grave in behalf of his child. But the crust of years was not to be so easily broken.

"Your father meant that I would look after you," she said, "and I mean to, but I can't afford to keep you here. You'll have a good place at Mr. Robins', if you behave yourself. I'm going to take you down now, before I unharness the pony, so go and wash your face while I put up your things. Don't look so woebegone, for pity's sake! I'm not taking you to prison."

Wilbur turned and went silently to the kitchen. Miss Cynthia thought she heard a sob. She went with a firm step into the little bedroom off the hall and took a purse out of a drawer.

"I s'pose I ought," she said doubtfully. "I don't s'pose he has a cent. I daresay he'll lose or waste it."

She counted out seventy-five cents carefully. When she came out, Wilbur was at the door. She put the money awkwardly into his hand.

"There, see that you don't spend it on any foolishness."

MISS CYNTHIA'S ACTION made a good deal of talk in Wilmot. The women, headed by Mrs. John Joe – who said behind Cynthia's back what she did not dare say to her face – condemned her. The men laughed and said that Cynthia was a shrewd one; there was no getting round her. Miss Cynthia herself was far from easy. She could not forget Wilbur's wistful eyes, and she had heard that Robins was a hard master.

A week after the boy had gone she saw him one day at the store. He was lifting heavy bags from a cart. The work was beyond his strength, and he was flushed and panting. Miss Cynthia's conscience gave her a hard stab. She bought a roll of peppermints and took them over to him. He thanked her timidly and drove quickly away.

"Robins hasn't any business putting such work on a child," she said to herself indignantly. "I'll speak to him about it."

And she did – and got an answer that made her ears tingle. Mr. Robins bluntly told her he guessed he knew what was what about his hands. He weren't no nigger driver. If she wasn't satisfied, she might take the boy away as soon as she liked.

Miss Cynthia did not get much comfort out of life that summer. Almost everywhere she went she was sure to meet Wilbur, engaged in some hard task. She could not help seeing how miserably pale and thin he had become. The worry had its effect on her. The neighbours said that Cynthy was sharper than ever. Even her church-going was embittered. She had always enjoyed walking up the aisle with her rich silk skirt rustling over the carpet, her cashmere shawl folded correctly over her shoulders, and her lace bonnet set precisely on her thin shining crimps. But she could take no pleasure in that or in the sermon now, when Wilbur sat right across from her pew, between hard-featured Robins and his sulky-looking wife. The boy's eyes had grown too large for his thin face.

The softening of Miss Cynthia was a very gradual process, but it reached a climax one September morning, when Mrs. John Joe came into the former's kitchen with an important face. Miss Cynthia was preserving her plums.

"No, thank you, I'll not sit down – I only run in – I suppose you've heard it. That little Merrivale boy has took awful sick with fever, they say. He's been worked half to death this summer – everyone knows what Robins is with his help – and they say he has fretted a good deal for his father and been homesick, and he's run down, I s'pose. Anyway, Robins took him over to the hospital at Stanford last night – good gracious, Cynthy, are you sick?"

Miss Cynthia had staggered to a seat by the table; her face was pallid.

"No, it's only your news gave me a turn – it came so suddenly – I didn't know."

"I must hurry back and see to the men's dinners. I thought I'd come and tell you, though I didn't know as you'd care."

This parting shot was unheeded by Miss Cynthia. She laid her face in her hands. "It's a judgement on me," she moaned. "He's going to die, and I'm his murderess. This is the account I'll have to give John Merrivale of his boy. I've been a wicked, selfish woman, and I'm justly punished."

It was a humbled Miss Cynthia who met the doctor at

the hospital that afternoon. He shook his head at her eager questions.

"It's a pretty bad case. The boy seems run down every way. No, it is impossible to think of moving him again. Bringing him here last night did him a great deal of harm. Yes, you may see him, but he will not know you, I fear – he is delirious and raves of his father and California."

Miss Cynthia followed the doctor down the long ward. When he paused by a cot, she pushed past him. Wilbur lay tossing restlessly on his pillow. He was thin to emaciation, but his cheeks were crimson and his eyes burning bright.

Miss Cynthia stooped and took the hot, dry hands in hers.

"Wilbur," she sobbed, "don't you know me – Aunt Cynthia?"

"You are not my Aunt Cynthia," said Wilbur. "Daddy said Aunt Cynthia was good and kind – you are a cross, bad woman. I want Daddy. Why doesn't he come? Why doesn't he come to little Wilbur?"

Miss Cynthia got up and faced the doctor.

"He's *got* to get better," she said stubbornly. "Spare no expense or trouble. If he dies, I will be a murderess. He must live and give me a chance to make it up for him."

And he did live; but for a long time it was a hard fight, and there were days when it seemed that death must win. Miss Cynthia got so thin and wan that even Mrs. John Joe pitied her.

The earth seemed to Miss Cynthia to laugh out in prodigal joyousness on the afternoon she drove home when Wilbur had been pronounced out of danger. How tranquil the hills looked, with warm October sunshine sleeping on their sides and faint blue hazes on their brows! How gallantly the maples flaunted their crimson flags! How kind and friendly was every face she met! Afterwards, Miss Cynthia said she began to live that day.

Wilbur's recovery was slow. Every day Miss Cynthia drove over with some dainty, and her loving gentleness sat none the less gracefully on her because of its newness. Wilbur grew to look for and welcome her coming. When it was thought safe to remove him, Miss Cynthia went to the hospital with a phaeton-load of shawls and pillows.

"I have come to take you away," she said.

Wilbur shrank back. "Not to Mr. Robins," he said piteously. "Oh, not there, Aunt Cynthia!"

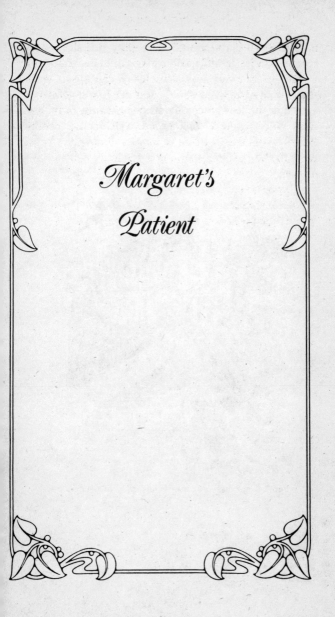

Margaret's
Patient

"DID DR. FORBES THINK SHE OUGHT TO GIVE UP HER TRIP?"

ARGARET paused a moment at the gate and looked back at the quaint old house under its snowy firs with a thrill of proprietary affection. It was her home; for the first time in her life she had a real home, and the long, weary years of poorly paid drudgery were all behind her. Before her was a prospect of independence and many of the delights she had always craved; in the immediate future was a trip to Vancouver with Mrs. Boyd.

For I shall go, of course, thought Margaret, as she walked briskly down the snowy road. I've always wanted to see the Rockies, and to go there with Mrs. Boyd will double the pleasure. She is such a delightful companion.

Margaret Campbell had been an orphan ever since she could remember. She had been brought up by a distant relative of her father's – that is, she had been given board, lodging, some schooling and indifferent clothes for the privilege of working like a little drudge in the house of the grim cousin who sheltered her. The death of this cousin flung Margaret on her own resources. A friend had procured her employment as the "companion" of a rich, eccentric old lady, infirm of health and temper. Margaret lived with her for five years, and to the young girl they seemed treble the time. Her employer was fault-finding, peevish, unreasonable, and many a time Margaret's patience almost failed her – almost, but not quite. In the end it brought her a more tangible reward than sometimes falls to the lot of the toiler. Mrs. Constance died, and in her will she left to Margaret her little up-country cottage and enough money to provide her an income for the rest of her life.

Margaret took immediate possession of her little house and, with the aid of a capable old servant, soon found herself very comfortable. She realized that her days of drudgery were over, and that henceforth life would be a very different thing from what it had been. Margaret meant to have "a good time." She had never had any pleasure and now she was resolved to garner in all she could of the joys of existence.

"I'm not going to do a single useful thing for a year," she had told Mrs. Boyd gaily. "Just think of it – a whole delightful year of vacation, to go and come at will, to read, travel, dream, rest. After that, I mean to see if I can find something to do for other folks, but I'm going to have this one golden year. And the first thing in it is our trip to Vancouver. I'm so glad I have the chance to go with you. It's a wee bit short notice, but I'll be ready when you want to start."

Altogether, Margaret felt pretty well satisfied with life as she tripped blithely down the country road between the ranks of snow-laden spruces, with the blue sky above and the crisp, exhilarating air all about. There was only one drawback, but it was a pretty serious one.

It's so lonely by spells, Margaret sometimes thought wistfully. All the joys my good fortune has brought me can't quite fill my heart. There's always one little empty, aching spot. Oh, if I had somebody of my very own to love and care for, a mother, a sister, even a cousin. But there's nobody. I haven't a relative in the world, and there are times when I'd give almost anything to have one. Well, I must try to be satisfied with friendship, instead.

Margaret's meditations were interrupted by a brisk footstep behind her, and presently Dr. Forbes came up.

"Good afternoon, Miss Campbell. Taking a constitutional?"

"Yes. Isn't it a lovely day? I suppose you are on your professional rounds. How are all your patients?"

"Most of them are doing well. But I'm sorry to say I

have a new one and am very much worried about her. Do you know Freda Martin?''

"The little teacher in the Primary Department who boards with the Wayes? Yes, I've met her once or twice. Is she ill?''

"Yes, seriously. It's typhoid, and she has been going about longer than she should. I don't know what is to be done with her. It seems she is like yourself in one respect, Miss Campbell; she is utterly alone in the world. Mrs. Waye is crippled with rheumatism and can't nurse her, and I fear it will be impossible to get a nurse in Blythefield. She ought to be taken from the Wayes'. The house is overrun with children, is right next door to that noisy factory, and in other respects is a poor place for a sick girl.''

"It is too bad, I am very sorry,'' said Margaret sympathetically.

Dr. Forbes shot a keen look at her from his deep-set eyes. "Are you willing to show your sympathy in a practical form, Miss Campbell?'' he said bluntly. "You told me the other day you meant to begin work for others next year. Why not begin now? Here's a splendid chance to befriend a friendless girl. Will you take Freda Martin into your home during her illness?''

"Oh, I couldn't,'' cried Margaret blankly. "Why, I'm going away next week. I'm going with Mrs. Boyd to Vancouver, and my house will be shut up.''

"Oh, I did not know. That settles it, I suppose,'' said the doctor with a sigh of regret. "Well, I must see what else I can do for poor Freda. If I had a home of my own, the problem would be easily solved, but as I'm only a boarder myself, I'm helpless in that respect. I'm very much afraid she will have a hard time to pull through, but I'll do the best I can for her. Well, I must run in here and have a look at Tommy Griggs' eyes. Good morning, Miss Campbell."

Margaret responded rather absently and walked on with her eyes fixed on the road. Somehow all the joy had gone out of the day for her, and out of her prospective trip. She stopped on the little bridge and gazed unseeingly at the ice-bound creek. Did Dr. Forbes really think she ought to give up her trip in order to take Freda Martin into her home and probably nurse her as well, since skilled nursing of any kind was almost unobtainable in Blythefield? No, of course, Dr. Forbes did not mean anything of the sort. He had not known she intended to go away. Margaret tried to put the thought out of her mind, but it came insistently back.

She knew – none better – what it was to be alone and friendless. Once she had been ill, too, and left to the ministration of careless servants. Margaret shuddered whenever she thought of that time. She was very, very sorry for Freda Martin, but she certainly couldn't give up her plans for her.

"Why, I'd never have the chance to go with Mrs. Boyd again," she argued with her troublesome inward promptings.

Altogether, Margaret's walk was spoiled. But when she went to bed that night, she was firmly resolved to dismiss all thought of Freda Martin. In the middle of the night she woke up. It was calm and moonlight and frosty. The world was very still, and Margaret's heart and conscience spoke to her out of that silence, where all worldly motives were hushed and shamed. She listened, and knew that in the morning she must send for Dr. Forbes and tell him to bring his patient to Fir Cottage.

The evening of the next day found Freda in Margaret's spare room and Margaret herself installed as nurse, for as Dr. Forbes had feared, he had found it impossible to obtain anyone else. Margaret had a natural gift for nursing, and she had had a good deal of experience in sick rooms. She was skilful, gentle and composed, and Dr. Forbes nodded his head with satisfaction as he watched her.

A week later Mrs. Boyd left for Vancouver, and Margaret, bending over her delirious patient, could not even go to the station to see her off. But she thought little about it. All her hopes were centred on pulling Freda Martin through; and when, after a long, doubtful fortnight, Dr. Forbes pronounced her on the way to recovery, Margaret felt as if she had given the gift of life to a fellow creature. "Oh, I am so glad I stayed," she whispered to herself.

During Freda's convalescence Margaret learned to love her dearly. She was such a sweet, brave little creature, full of a fine courage to face the loneliness and trials of her lot.

"I can never repay you for your kindness, Miss Campbell," she said wistfully.

"I am more than repaid already," said Margaret sincerely. "Haven't I found a dear little friend?"

One day Freda asked Margaret to write a note for her to a certain school chum.

"She will like to know I am getting better. You will find her address in my writing desk."

Freda's modest trunk had been brought to Fir Cottage, and Margaret went to it for the desk. As she turned over the loose papers in search of the address, her eye was caught by a name signed to a faded and yellowed letter – Worth Spencer. Her mother's name!

Margaret gave a little exclamation of astonishment. Could her mother have written that letter? It was not likely another woman would have that uncommon name. Margaret caught up the letter and ran to Freda's room.

"Freda, I couldn't help seeing the name signed to this letter, it is my mother's. To whom was it written?"

"That is one of my mother's old letters," said Freda. "She had a sister, my Aunt Worth. She was a great deal older than Mother. Their parents died when Mother was a baby. Aunt Worth went to her father's people, while Mother's grandmother took her. There was not very good feeling between the two families, I think. Mother said she lost trace of her sister after her sister married, and then, long after, she saw Aunt Worth's death in the papers."

"Can you tell me where your mother and her sister lived before they were separated?" asked Margaret excitedly.

"Ridgetown."

"Then my mother must have been your mother's sister, and, oh, Freda, Freda, you are my cousin."

Eventually this was proved to be the fact. Margaret investigated the matter and discovered beyond a doubt that she and Freda were cousins. It would be hard to say which of the two girls was the more delighted.

"Anyhow, we'll never be parted again," said Margaret happily. "Fir Cottage is your home henceforth, Freda. Oh, how rich I am. I have got somebody who really belongs to me. And I owe it all to Dr. Forbes. If he hadn't suggested you coming here, I should never have found out that we were cousins."

"And I don't think I should ever have got better at all," whispered Freda, slipping her hand into Margaret's.

"I think we are going to be the two happiest girls in the world," said Margaret. "And Freda, do you know what we are going to do when your summer vacation comes? We are going to have a trip through the Rockies, yes, indeedy. It would have been nice going with Mrs. Boyd, but it will be ten times nicer to go with you."

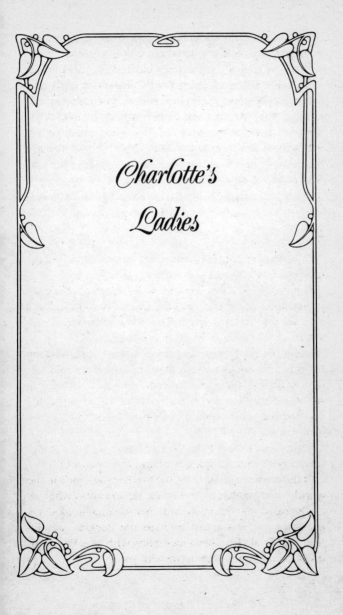

Charlotte's

Ladies

UST AS SOON AS dinner was over at the asylum, Charlotte sped away to the gap in the fence – the northwest corner gap. There was a gap in the southeast corner, too – the asylum fence *was* in a rather poor condition – but the southeast gap was interesting only after tea, and it was never at any time quite as interesting as the northwest gap.

Charlotte ran as fast as her legs could carry her, for she did not want any of the other orphans to see her. As a rule, Charlotte liked the company of the other orphans and was a favourite with them. But, somehow, she did not want them to know about the gaps. She was sure they would not understand.

Charlotte had discovered the gaps only a week before. They had not been there in the autumn, but the snow-drifts had lain heavily against the fence all winter, and one spring day when Charlotte was creeping through the shrubbery in the northwest corner in search of the little yellow daffodils that always grew there in spring, she found a delightful space where a board had fallen off, whence she could look out on a bit of woodsy road with a little footpath winding along by the fence under the widespreading boughs of the asylum trees. Charlotte felt a wild impulse to slip out and run fast and far down that lovely, sunny, tempting, fenceless road. But that would have been wrong, for it was against the asylum rules, and Charlotte, though she hated most of the asylum rules with all her heart, never disobeyed or broke them. So she subdued the vagrant longing with a sigh and sat down among the daffodils to peer wistfully out of the gap and feast her eyes on this glimpse of a world where there were no brick walls and prim walks and never-varying rules.

Then, as Charlotte watched, the Pretty Lady with the

Blue Eyes came along the footpath. Charlotte had never seen her before and hadn't the slightest idea in the world who she was, but that was what she called her as soon as she saw her. The lady was so pretty, with lovely blue eyes that were very sad, although somehow as you looked at them you felt that they ought to be laughing, merry eyes instead. At least Charlotte thought so and wished at once that she knew how to make them laugh. Besides, the Lady had lovely golden hair and the most beautiful pink cheeks, and Charlotte, who had mouse-coloured hair and any number of freckles, had an unbounded admiration for golden locks and roseleaf complexions. The Lady was dressed in black, which Charlotte didn't like, principally because the matron of the asylum wore black and Charlotte didn't – exactly – like the matron.

When the Pretty Lady with the Blue Eyes had gone by, Charlotte drew a long breath.

"If I could pick out a mother I'd pick out one that looked just like her," she said.

Nice things sometimes happen close together, even in an orphan asylum, and that very evening Charlotte discovered the southeast gap and found herself peering into the most beautiful garden you could imagine, a garden where daffodils and tulips grew in great ribbon-like beds, and there were hedges of white and purple lilacs, and winding paths under blossoming trees. It was such a garden as Charlotte had pictured in happy dreams and never expected to see in real life. And yet here it had been all the time, divided from her only by a high board fence.

"I wouldn't have s'posed there could be such a lovely place so near an orphan asylum," mused Charlotte. "It's the very loveliest place I ever saw. Oh, I do wish I could go and walk in it. Well, I do declare! If there isn't a lady in it, too!"

Sure enough, there was a lady, helping an unruly young vine to run in the way it should go over a little arbour. Charlotte instantly named her the Tall Lady with the Black Eyes. She was not nearly so young or so pretty as the Lady with the Blue Eyes, but she looked very kind and jolly.

I'd like her for an aunt, reflected Charlotte. Not for a mother – oh, no, not for a mother, but for an aunt. I know she'd make a splendid aunt. And, oh, just look at her cat!

Charlotte looked at the cat with all her might and main. She loved cats, but cats were not allowed in an orphan asylum, although Charlotte sometimes wondered if there were no orphan kittens in the world which would be appropriate for such an institution.

The Tall Lady's cat was so big and furry, with a splendid tail and elegant stripes. A Very Handsome Cat, Charlotte called him mentally, seeing the capitals as plainly as if they had been printed out. Charlotte's fingers tingled to stroke his glossy coat, but she folded them sternly together.

"You know you can't," she said to herself reproachfully, "so what is the use of wanting to, Charlotte Turner? You ought to be thankful just to *see* the garden and the Very Handsome Cat."

Charlotte watched the Tall Lady and the Cat until they went away into a fine, big house further up the garden, then she sighed and went back through the cherry trees to the asylum playground, where the other orphans were playing games. But, somehow, games had lost their flavour compared with those fascinating gaps.

It did not take Charlotte long to discover that the Pretty Lady always walked past the northwest gap about one o'clock every day and never at any other time – at least at no other time when Charlotte was free to watch her; and that the Tall Lady was almost always in her garden at five in the afternoon, accompanied by the Very Handsome Cat, pruning and trimming some of her flowers. Charlotte never missed being at the gaps at the proper times, if she could possibly manage it, and her heart was full of dreams about her two Ladies. But the other orphans thought all the fun had gone out of her, and the matron noticed her absent-mindedness and dosed her with sulphur and molasses for it. Charlotte took the dose meekly, as she took everything else. It was all part and parcel with being an orphan in an asylum.

"But if the Pretty Lady with the Blue Eyes was my mother, she wouldn't make me swallow such dreadful stuff," sighed Charlotte. "I don't believe even the Tall Lady with the Black Eyes would – though perhaps she might, aunts not being quite as good as mothers."

"Do you know," said Maggie Brunt, coming up to Charlotte at this moment, "that Lizzie Parker is going to be adopted? A lady is going to adopt her."

"Oh!" cried Charlotte breathlessly. An adoption was always a wonderful event in the asylum, as well as a somewhat rare one. "Oh, how splendid!"

"Yes, isn't it?" said Maggie enviously. "She picked out Lizzie because she was pretty and had curls. I don't think it is fair."

Charlotte sighed. "Nobody will ever want to adopt me, because I've mousy hair and freckles," she said. "But somebody may want you some day, Maggie. You have such lovely black hair."

"But it isn't curly," said Maggie forlornly. "And the matron won't let me put it up in curl papers at night. I just wish I was Lizzie."

Charlotte shook her head. "I don't. I'd love to be adopted, but I wouldn't really like to be anybody but myself, even if I am homely. It's better to be yourself with mousy hair and freckles than somebody else who is ever so beautiful. But I do envy Lizzie, though the matron says it is wicked to envy anyone."

Envy of the fortunate Lizzie did not long possess Charlotte's mind, however, for that very day a wonderful thing happened at noon hour by the northwest gap. Charlotte had always been very careful not to let the Pretty Lady see her, but today, after the Pretty Lady had gone past, Charlotte leaned out of the gap to watch her as far as she could. And just at that very moment the Pretty Lady looked back; and there, peering at her from the asylum fence, was a little scrap of a girl, with mouse-coloured hair and big freckles, and the sweetest, brightest, most winsome little face the Pretty Lady had ever seen. The Pretty Lady smiled right down at Charlotte and for just a moment her eyes looked as Charlotte had always known they ought to look. Charlotte was feeling rather frightened down in her heart but she smiled bravely back.

"Are you thinking of running away?" said the Pretty Lady, and, oh, what a sweet voice she had – sweet and tender, just like a mother's voice ought to be!

"No," said Charlotte, shaking her head gravely. "I should like to run away but it would be of no use, because there is no place to run to."

"Why would you like to run away?" asked the Pretty Lady, still smiling. "Don't you like living here?"

Charlotte opened her big eyes very widely. "Why, it's an orphan asylum!" she exclaimed. "Nobody could like living in an orphan asylum. But, of course, orphans should be very thankful to have any place to live in and I *am* thankful. I'd be thankfuller still if the matron wouldn't make me take sulphur and molasses. If you had a little girl, would you make her take sulphur and molasses?"

"I didn't when I had a little girl," said the Pretty Lady wistfully, and her eyes were sad again.

"Oh, did you really have a little girl once?" asked Charlotte softly.

"Yes, and she died," said the Pretty Lady in a trembling voice.

"Oh, I am sorry," said Charlotte, more softly still. "Did she – did she have lovely golden hair and pink cheeks like yours?"

"No," the Pretty Lady smiled again, though it was a very sad smile. "No, she had mouse-coloured hair and freckles."

"Oh! And weren't you sorry?"

"No, I was glad of it, because it made her look like her father. I've always loved little girls with mouse-coloured hair and freckles ever since. Well, I must hurry along. I'm late now, and schools have a dreadful habit of going in sharp on time. If you should happen to be here tomorrow, I'm going to stop and ask your name."

Of course Charlotte was at the gap the next day and they had a lovely talk. In a week they were the best of friends. Charlotte soon found out that she could make the Pretty Lady's eyes look as they ought to for a little while at least, and she spent all her spare time and lay awake at nights devising speeches to make the Pretty Lady laugh.

Then another wonderful thing happened. One evening when Charlotte went to the southeast gap, the Tall Lady with the Black Eyes was not in the garden – at least, Charlotte thought she wasn't. But the Very Handsome Cat was, sitting gravely under a syringa bush and looking quite proud of himself for being a cat.

"You Very Handsome Cat," said Charlotte, "won't you come here and let me stroke you?"

The Very Handsome Cat did come, just as if he understood English, and he purred with delight when Charlotte took him in her arms and buried her face in his fur. Then – Charlotte thought she would really sink into the ground, for the Tall Lady herself came around a lilac bush and stood before the gap.

"Please, ma'am," stammered Charlotte in an agony of embarrassment, "I wasn't meaning to do any harm to your Very Handsome Cat. I just wanted to pat him. I – I am very fond of cats and they are not allowed in orphan asylums."

"I've always thought asylums weren't run on proper principles," said the Tall Lady briskly. "Bless your heart, child, don't look so scared. You're welcome to pat the cat all you like. Come in and I'll give you some flowers."

"Thank you, but I am not allowed to go off the grounds," said Charlotte firmly, "and I think I'd rather not have any flowers because the matron might want to know where I got them, and then she would have this gap closed up. I live in mortal dread for fear it will be closed anyhow. It's very uncomfortable – living in mortal dread."

The Tall Lady laughed a very jolly laugh. "Yes, I should think it would be," she agreed. "I haven't had that experience."

Then they had a jolly talk, and every evening after that Charlotte went to the gap and stroked the Very Handsome Cat and chatted to the Tall Lady.

"Do you live all alone in that big house?" she asked wonderingly one day.

"All alone," said the Tall Lady.

"Did you always live alone?"

"No. I had a sister living with me once. But I don't want to talk about her. You'll oblige me, Charlotte, by *not* talking about her."

"I won't then," agreed Charlotte. "I can understand

why people don't like to have their sisters talked about sometimes. Lily Mitchell has a big sister who was sent to jail for stealing. Of course Lily doesn't like to talk about her."

The Tall Lady laughed a little bitterly. "My sister didn't steal. She married a man I detested, that's all."

"Did he drink?" asked Charlotte gravely. "The matron's husband drank and that was why she left him and took to running an orphan asylum. I think I'd rather put up with a drunken husband than live in an orphan asylum."

"My sister's husband didn't drink," said the Tall Lady grimly. "He was beneath her, that was all. I told her I'd never forgive her and I never shall. He's dead now – he died a year after she married him – and she's working for her living. I dare say she doesn't find it very pleasant. She wasn't brought up to that. Here, Charlotte, is a turnover for you. I made it on purpose for you. Eat it and tell me if you don't think I'm a good cook. I'm dying for a compliment. I never get any now that I've got old. It's a dismal thing to get old and have nobody to love you except a cat, Charlotte."

"I think it is just as bad to be young and have nobody to love you, not *even* a cat," sighed Charlotte, enjoying the turnover, nevertheless.

"I dare say it is," agreed the Tall Lady, looking as if she had been struck by a new and rather startling idea.

I LIKE THE TALL LADY with the Black Eyes ever so much, thought Charlotte that night as she lay in bed, but I love the Pretty Lady. I have more fun with the Tall Lady and the Very Handsome Cat, but I always feel nicer with the Pretty Lady. Oh, I'm so glad her little girl had mouse-coloured hair.

Then the most wonderful thing of all happened. One

day a week later the Pretty Lady said, "Would you like to come and live with me, Charlotte?"

Charlotte looked at her. "Are you in earnest?" she asked in a whisper.

"Indeed I am. I want you for my little girl, and if you'd like to come, you shall. I'm poor, Charlotte, really, I'm dreadfully poor, but I can make my salary stretch far enough for two, and we'll love each other enough to cover the thin spots. Will you come?"

"Well, I should just think I will!" said Charlotte emphatically. "Oh, I wish I was sure I'm not dreaming. I do love you so much, and it will be so delightful to be your little girl."

"Very well, sweetheart. I'll come tomorrow afternoon – it is Saturday, so I'll have the whole blessed day off – and see the matron about it. Oh, we'll have lovely times together, dearest. I only wish I'd discovered you long ago."

Charlotte may have eaten and studied and played and kept rules the rest of that day and part of the next, but, if so, she has no recollection of it. She went about like a girl in a dream, and the matron concluded that something more than sulphur and molasses was needed and decided to speak to the doctor about her. But she never did, because a lady came that afternoon and told her she wanted to adopt Charlotte.

Charlotte obeyed the summons to the matron's room in a tingle of excitement. But when she went in, she saw only the matron and the Tall Lady with the Black Eyes. Before Charlotte could look around for the Pretty Lady the matron said, "Charlotte, this lady, Miss Herbert, wishes to adopt you. It is a splendid thing for you, and you ought to be a very thankful little girl."

Charlotte's head fairly whirled. She clasped her hands and the tears brimmed up in her eyes.

"Oh, I like the Tall Lady," she gasped, "but I *love* the Pretty Lady and I promised her I'd be her little girl. I can't break my promise."

"What on earth is the child talking about?" said the mystified matron.

And just then the maid showed in the Pretty Lady. Charlotte flew to her and flung her arms about her.

"Oh, tell them I am your little girl!" she begged. "Tell them I promised you first. I don't want to hurt the Tall Lady's feelings because I truly do like her so very much. But I want to be your little girl."

The Pretty Lady had given one glance at the Tall Lady and flushed red. The Tall Lady, on the contrary, had grown very pale. The matron felt uncomfortable. Everybody knew that Miss Herbert and Mrs. Bond hadn't spoken to each other for years, even if they were sisters and alone in the world except for each other.

Mrs. Bond turned to the matron. "I have come to ask permission to adopt this little girl," she said.

"Oh, I'm very sorry," stammered the matron, "but Miss Herbert has just asked for her, and I have consented."

Charlotte gave a great gulp of disappointment, but the Pretty Lady suddenly wheeled around to face the Tall Lady, with quivering lips and tearful eyes.

"Don't take her from me, Alma," she pleaded humbly. "She – she is so like my own baby and I'm so lonely. Any other child will suit you as well."

"Not at all," said the Tall Lady brusquely. "Not at all, Anna. No other child will suit me at all. And may I ask what you intend to keep her on? I know your salary is barely enough for yourself."

"That is my concern," said the Pretty Lady a little proudly.

"Humph!" The Tall Lady shrugged her shoulders. "Just as independent as ever, Anna, I see. Well, child, what do *you* say? Which of us will you come with? Remember, I have the cat on my side, and Anna can't make half as good turnovers as I can. Remember all this, Charlotte."

"Oh, I – I like you so much," stammered Charlotte, "and I wish I could live with you both. But since I can't, I must go with the Pretty Lady, because I promised, and because I loved her first."

"And best?" queried the Tall Lady.

"And best," admitted Charlotte, bound to be truthful, even at the risk of hurting the Tall Lady's feelings. "But I *do* like you, too – next best. And you really don't need me as much as she does, for you have your Very Handsome Cat and she hasn't anything."

"A cat no longer satisfies the aching void in my soul," said the Tall Lady stubbornly. "Nothing will satisfy it but a little girl with mouse-coloured hair and freckles. No, Anna, I've got to have Charlotte. But I think that with her usual astuteness, she has already solved the problem for us by saying she'd like to live with us both. Why can't she? You just come back home and we'll let bygones be bygones. We both have something to forgive, but I was an obstinate old fool and I've known it for years, though I never confessed it to anybody but the cat."

The Pretty Lady softened, trembled, smiled. She went right up to the Tall Lady and put her arms about her neck.

"Oh, I've wanted so much to be friends with you again," she sobbed. "But I thought you would never re-lent – and – and – I've been so lonely –"

"There, there," whispered the Tall Lady, "don't cry under the matron's eye. Wait till we get home. I may have some crying to do myself then. Charlotte, go and get your hat and come right over with us. We can sign the necessary papers later on, but we must have you right off. The cat is waiting for you on the back porch, and there is a turnover cooling on the pantry window that is just your size."

"I am so happy," remarked Charlotte, "that I feel like crying myself."

Editorial Note

These stories were originally published in the following magazines and newspapers, and are listed in the order of appearance in this collection. Where the original illustrations accompanying the stories are available, they have been included. Obvious typographical errors have been corrected, spelling and punctuation normalized.

Charlotte's Quest, *Family Herald*, January 1933.

Marcella's Reward, *Zion's Herald*, August 1907.

An Invitation Given on Impulse, *Philadelphia Times*, April 1900.

Freda's Adopted Grave, *Zion's Herald*, September 1904.

Ted's Afternoon Off, *King's Own*, August 1907.

The Girl Who Drove the Cows, *Presbyterian Banner*, October 1908.

Why Not Ask Miss Price? *Girls' Companion*, November 1904.

Jane Lavinia, *Zion's Herald*, September 1906.

The Running Away of Chester, *Boys' World*, November-December 1903.

Millicent's Double, *East and West*, December 1905.

Penelope's Party Waist, *Designer*, March 1904.

The Little Black Doll, *Zion's Herald*, August 1909.

The Fraser Scholarship, *Boys' World*, April 1905.

Her Own People, *American Messenger*, August 1905.

Miss Sally's Company, *Forward*, October 1904.

The Story of an Invitation, *Philadelphia Times*, August 1901.

The Softening of Miss Cynthia, *Living Church*, July 1904.

Margaret's Patient, *East and West*, February 1908.

Charlotte's Ladies, *Epworth Herald*, February 1911.

Acknowledgements

The late Dr. Stuart Macdonald gave me permission to begin the research that culminated in this collection; Professors Mary Rubio and Elizabeth Waterston encouraged me; Professor C. Anderson Silber gave his always constant support. Librarians of all the libraries I used were unfailingly helpful.

OTHER BOOKS BY

L. M. Montgomery

For the most complete listing, see Russell, Russell, and Wilmshurst, *Lucy Maud Montgomery: A Preliminary Bibliography*, University of Waterloo Library Bibliography Series, No. 13 (Waterloo: University of Waterloo Library, 1986).

THE "ANNE" BOOKS (in order of Anne's life)

Anne of Green Gables, 1908
Anne of Avonlea, 1909
Anne of the Island, 1915
Anne of Windy Poplars, 1936
Anne's House of Dreams, 1917
Anne of Ingleside, 1939
Rainbow Valley, 1919
Rilla of Ingleside, 1920

THE "EMILY" BOOKS

Emily of New Moon, 1923
Emily Climbs, 1925
Emily's Quest, 1927

OTHER NOVELS (in chronological order)

Kilmeny of the Orchard, 1910
The Story Girl, 1911
The Golden Road, 1913
The Blue Castle, 1926
Magic for Marigold, 1929
A Tangled Web, 1931
Pat of Silver Bush, 1933
Mistress Pat, 1935
Jane of Lantern Hill, 1937

COLLECTIONS OF SHORT STORIES

Chronicles of Avonlea, 1912
Further Chronicles of Avonlea, 1920
The Road to Yesterday, 1974
The Doctor's Sweetheart, and Other Stories, 1979

POETRY

The Watchman, and Other Poems, 1916
Poetry of Lucy Maud Montgomery, 1987